Something Like a Love Affair

SOMETHING LIKE A LOVE AFFAIR

JULIAN SYMONS

Mys

THE MYSTERIOUS PRESS
New York • Tokyo • Sweden
Published by Warner Books

 A Time Warner Company

First published in 1992 by Macmillan London Limited, a division of Pan Macmillan Publishers Limited.

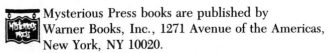Mysterious Press books are published by Warner Books, Inc., 1271 Avenue of the Americas, New York, NY 10020.

A Time Warner Company

Printed in the United States of America

First U.S. printing: February 1993

10   9   8   7   6   5   4   3   2   1

Library of Congress Cataloging in Publication Data

Symons, Julian
    Something like a love affair / Julian Symons.
        p.   cm.
    ISBN 0-89296-495-2
    I. Title.
    PR6037.Y5S66   1992
    823'.912—dc20   92-5980
                                                                                CIP

For Gavin Ewart

"Tomorrow for the young the poets exploding like bombs."
Like many tomorrows, that one never came.
Yet still, in this elderly today, you smilingly
Give poetry a shape, a rhyme, a name.

CONTENTS

AFTERWARDS

I say it was a body." At the suggestion of disbelief, the old man seemed to bristle all over. Hair shot out from the sides and back of the ridiculous cap he wore, his grey moustache bristled, the hairs on the back of his liver-spotted hands seemed to stand up. He quivered slightly with indignation at the doubt he sensed in the Duty Sergeant's manner. "A dead body," he added unnecessarily.

The Duty Sergeant spoke with elaborate politeness. "Look, Mr. Gant—"

"The name is Harrison Gant. As I have told your man before."

The large mouthful of name was too much for the Duty Sergeant, who merely nodded. "A month ago you reported a fire at a house in Heathfield Way, said you saw flames coming from the chimney and inside the house. Turned out the residents were having a barbecue and had poured oil on the brazier by mistake."

"Flames as high as the house."

1

"But not inside the house as you said. They coped with it themselves perfectly well."

"No trouble for you."

"A call-out for the Fire Department. And there's been some trouble for us since then as you may remember." He looked down at the papers in front of him. "Report of a burglar breaking and entering, Mallam Road. Turned out to be a householder lost his keys. Report of a woman attacked in Langley Street—"

"She was being attacked."

"Husband and wife squabble. She was *not*, as you said, bleeding and unconscious. On the contrary, she punched an officer in the stomach when he arrived, then scratched his face."

The old man folded his arms. "I do my duty as a citizen."

"I'm sure you do. Now, tell me about this body."

"It's my habit to take an evening constitutional. Clears the head, keeps the mind alert, good for the body. I vary my walk, and tonight went up to Burley Common. I took a road leading to St. Anselm's Church, taking me through a small wooded area—"

"Known locally as Lover's Lane," the Duty Sergeant said, with a careful lack of expression.

"Not aware of that. The body was a bit off the road, almost in a little ditch. Concealed, you might say."

"But still you found it. What made you leave the road?"

"What does it matter?" The old man bristled again. "Call of nature, if you must know. Then I stumbled across this body."

"Did you have a torch?"

"A small torch, yes."

"You shone it on the body?"

For the first time Harrison Gant showed uneasiness. "What's the meaning of that, what are you suggesting?"

The Duty Sergeant sighed, "Look, Mr. Harrison Gant, I'm

2

trying to make sure you're not wasting our time as you have done before. If you were close enough to shine a torch on this body and maybe touch it, that's one thing. If you shone it just for a moment or two from several feet away, what you saw is just guesswork. Now, which was it?"

The old man took off his cap. The hair beneath it sprang up. "I didn't come here to be insulted. I've reported what I saw, and done my citizen's duty. If you ignore it, young man, you'll find yourself in trouble." He put the cap on again, about-turned and walked out.

The Duty Sergeant logged the visit in a couple of lines, with the time: 9:40 p.m. It was a busy night at Wyfleet station, with a couple of household burglaries, an affray outside a pub and an attempted break-in at a factory, and although the Duty Sergeant told PC Lewis to check on the report, it was in terms that made it clear he had no faith in its accuracy. He said to Lewis, who was not the brightest figure on the payroll: "Had that bloody old fool Gant in again. He's been sniffing round the courting couples on Burley Common from the sound of it, thinks he saw a body. Somewhere off Lover's Lane. Twenty to one it was a couple in a clinch, he shone his torch, they scared him off and he's just being gabby, hopes they're still at it and we'll sort 'em out. But twenty to one outsiders do turn up sometimes, go down there, have a gander."

"Will do, Sarge." PC Lewis did have a look, and sure enough disturbed a courting couple half hidden under one of the bushes that almost bordered the narrow road. The man swore at him, Lewis told them they were committing an offence but he'd overlook it on this occasion, returned to his panda and described in detail what he had seen to his partner PC Bacon. When they had finished laughing they tooted goodbye and went on their way, reporting back that they had found Harrison Gant's "body," and that it was two not one.

Because of this the body was not found until morning, when

a woman taking a short cut on her way to an early morning factory shift saw it, turned it over, and then telephoned the police from a house nearby. By the time they arrived on the scene a husband and wife taking their dog for a pre-breakfast walk had seen it, and the earth and grass nearby was thoroughly trodden down.

PART ONE

Judith Alone

1

There were times when Judith Lassiter felt like two people. This happened especially in the morning when she was preparing breakfast. She carried this out with perfect efficiency, warming Victor's two croissants in the oven and then wrapping them in a napkin so that they should be as he liked them, not hot but with a memory of heat, doing her own toast to a dark brown colour so that it was almost but not quite burnt. Butter pats were neatly curled, apricot jam and the honey Victor sometimes preferred on the table, coffee ready by the hot-plate. All this was done each morning, but then she sometimes found herself looking down at her thin hands and moving the fingers with a feeling of wonder that they had once again obeyed her instructions. Or she was standing beside the sliding window that looked on to the garden's weedless paths and tidy flower beds, murmuring without knowing what she meant by the words: "Judith alone."

On this fine early June morning, she brought in the letters, sorting them as she always did. For Victor there was junk mail, a letter from the bank and one from Group Southeast, an architectural cooperative he belonged to which exchanged information about possible building developments in the area. For her there was one letter, the address written in a firm angular hand, the postmark local. She put this beside her plate so that it was not obvious but still not concealed. Then she drew her dressing gown round her, shivered slightly in spite of the day's warmth, poured herself coffee, and waited for Victor.

He came along the corridor that ran from the other end of the bungalow to this L-shaped living room with its separate eating area, divisible from the rest of the room by the metal wall looking like a curtain that came down at the touch of a button. His step was brisk, his blue jacket neat, his variously striped bow tie offered a deliberate touch of the unconventional. As he poured coffee, sat down, looked at his letters, she considered how that other person, Judith alone, might see him if he were not *my husband Victor*. The unsparing eye of Judith alone might have discerned a man a little under the proper size, no taller than herself, wonderfully neat, dapper, almost always cheerful, unable to pass a looking glass without regarding himself, forever passing a hand through his thick mouse-coloured hair, or touching the streak of his moustache as if to assure himself he was still there. That was the outer man. What would Judith say about the inner one? Nothing at all, for she would be unsure whether such a man existed. Then in a moment, as darkness cancels the picture on a television screen at the touch of a switch, those thoughts vanished, were replaced by the actuality of the man who sat opposite her across the breakfast table, the man whose life was linked to hers.

Victor ate honey with the first croissant, jam with the second. He took no butter, and she remarked on this.

"Seem to have put on a couple of pounds, got to be careful." His blue eyes, laughing eyes she had called them in the past, considered her. "You've no need to worry. Or to eat burnt toast."

"It's not burnt, just crisp. And I eat it that way because I like it."

"The best of reasons." The laughing eyes still considered her. Was her appearance some kind of joke? Perhaps it is, she thought, perhaps an untidy woman in a dressing gown seems a joke to a neat man wearing a striped bow tie. She realized she had missed something Victor had said.

"I asked if you had any post."

"A letter." She indicated where it lay, unopened, beside her plate. "Nothing important." Would he ask her to open it? But she knew he would not. No doubt he would feel he shouldn't pry. Instead he said he had a busy day ahead, asked what she was doing, nodded when she said she was meeting Debbie for lunch and then going on to the shop.

"Don't forget we're going out this evening."

"Must we?"

"Afraid so. Wheels within wheels. Some interesting people." He modified this. "One or two." Then hesitated. "Sorry it's this evening." He kissed her, was gone. Moments later she saw the Lagonda drifting down the steep drive. As often, Victor went down a little too quickly, had to break sharply when he reached the road.

She savoured for a few moments the feeling of being truly alone, then poured a second cup of coffee and looked at the paper. Victor took *The Times* to the office, leaving her with the tabloid. In the Middle East an Israeli bus had been stoned, the driver hit, the bus had run off the road, twenty-three people were injured. Three soldiers had been killed in West Belfast when a bomb exploded. At home a Greek had been knifed at a Polish dance, something to do with a shared girl friend. A rock star was on trial accused of luring two girls up to his flat, giving them drugs and raping them. A Birmingham man was on trial accused of hiring a hit man to kill his wife. A man living on social security had died and left an estate worth a quarter of a million pounds.

She read these stories, interested particularly for some reason by the one about the hit man. The husband was supposed to have told an acquaintance he was bored with his wife and wished something would happen to her. If she had an accident, he would give a hundred pounds to any charity.

"How did you interpret that?" the prosecuting counsel asked the witness, whose name was Wimbly. The witness said he took it to be a suggestion he should arrange the accident. "And that you would be the so-called charity?" The witness agreed. "What was your reaction?"

"I said I wouldn't consider it."

"And did you then put him in touch with a friend of yours?" Wimbly said his friend happened to be in the pub where they were talking. The case continued.

Judith wondered whether Victor was bored with her. She sighed, picked up the still unopened letter, and walked along the corridor, without pausing to look at Victor's watercolour sketches done on holidays in Tuscany, Sicily and northern Spain, to her bedroom, which adjoined his. She glanced at his room, taking in the school photographs on the wall and the family group showing Victor as a teenager standing between his anxious-looking mother and the Old Man, whose hand rested firmly on his son's shoulder. There were other photographs in which Judith appeared, a wedding picture, the two of them beside an old but remarkably durable car somewhere near Vigo, but it was that one of the Old Man's proprietorial hand on his son's shoulder over which she lingered. Apart from the photographs Victor's room was bare and bleak, curtains and bed cover stone grey, cupboard and chest of drawers unvarnished pine. A bedroom, Victor said, should be functional, offer no distraction. As if in defiance of his creed, although that was not her conscious intention, her room was rich with shape and colour, a strong flower pattern in the wallpaper repeated with variations in the skirts of the dressing table and the quilted bed cover. There were no photographs, but Seurat and Monet prints on the walls, chosen because the colours fitted those of the paper. She would have liked Victor to say what he thought of the decoration, to be critical or even scornful, but he had smiled, stroked his little moustache and said it was her choice. They had occupied separate rooms since the bungalow had been built to his design seven years ago.

She put the letter on the dressing table, went into her bathroom which like the bedroom was a little smaller than Victor's, removed dressing gown and nightdress and considered her body while she ran a bath. "A good figure," she said aloud, and approved the small but not sagging breasts, ran a hand down the long lean legs, momentarily touched her vagina, shuddered.

Twenty minutes later she was out of the bath and dressed. It was time for the letter. She allowed imagination to play over what her reaction would have been if Victor had insisted she open the letter in front of him, demanded to read it. To have left it on the breakfast table was a kind of dare, but one she knew involved no risk, since it would have been against Victor's nature to have made such a demand.

She opened the letter, read the first lines:

> Dearest, sweetest coz,
> These days since we parted have been beyond bear-
> ing. I have longed for the electric thrill in the touch
> of your hand, ached to hold you in my arms again,
> and hear you murmur the words dearer to me than
> any others, saying oh my darling, my beautiful pas-
> sionate darling, the incredible words that you love me.

There were two more pages, pages in which the angular writing changed, so that by the end the signature "Philo" more nearly resembled her own hand. The letter came from *The Lord of Courtney Castle*, one of the romantic historical novels she had been reading voraciously for the past twelve months, and was the third she had sent to herself. She read it through, said "I must be going crackers," tore the letter and envelope into small pieces and put them in the wastepaper basket. A clattering of plates and dishes below, blending with yells and screeches that could come only from the TV, told her Patty had arrived and Derek was with her. She prepared to face the day.

Victor had named the bungalow Green Diamonds, after the glittering green diamond-shaped tiles used on his instructions for the roof. It was an American ranch-style house, built on a piece of high land that formed a small plateau below which the earth shelved sharply, so that from the deck outside the living room there was a view beyond the small neat lawn and the flowerbeds of Sussex fields and the steel gleam of a river winding in S bends towards the sea several miles away. The Old Man had approved the siting of the bungalow and its position nearly a mile out of town but had condemned the glittering tiles as a piece of vulgarity. Did Victor deliberately invite his father's disapproval by this tiny mark of rebellion? She sometimes thought so.

Patty was an unmarried mother in her very early twenties. She lived in a conglomeration of streets and houses built a few years ago and named the Orchard Estate, but never called anything but the Estate. She had a council house which also housed her lover Rocky and her five-year-old Derek, who was her child by somebody named Carl. Rocky was a long-distance lorry driver who seemed to spend a good deal of time at home. When he was taking a load to Lyons or Amsterdam or Warsaw it seemed that Carl moved in. Where he lived when Rocky was in occupation, and what, if any, work he did, remained a mystery to Judith. It was not that Patty, a frizzy-haired amiable girl, was unwilling to talk about her men, but her tales of their activities and the roles they played in her life were so unlike anything Judith had known that she seemed at times to be hearing accounts of people of a different species. Today as they sat drinking instant coffee Judith learned Carl was not as she had supposed, a German, and that that was not his name.

"He got it because, you know, he was in this group and

they were the Fighting Foreigners, gave themselves names like Carl and Anders and, you know, Franz and Gerhart and that, and there was a girl called Lena, and they used to throw stuff around and fight like, you know, it was part of their act. They wore uniforms and saluted and that. Course, the trouble was none of 'em could sing."

"So what's Carl's real name?"

Patty looked surprised. "I dunno, do I? I mean it's what I always called him, Carl."

"And what does he do now?"

"Just sort of odd jobs, you know, depends what turns up, he'd done all sorts."

"Driving a lorry?"

"Nothing like that, wouldn't dirty his hands, Carl." She gave a delighted giggle at the idea. "He was in advertising for a bit, making up rhymes and stuff. On the stage too, I mean the real stage not just the Fighting Foreigners and that. Not like Rocky, Rocky's thick. He's lovely, though. Not like Carl."

"Carl isn't lovely?"

It was not easy for Patty to look troubled, but she almost managed it. "He can be, you know, nasty. Specially with Derek. What I mean is you'd think Carl being his dad and that it would be all right, but it's not. Rocky, you see, he's as good as gold with Rocky. Course kids are a bother, but you wouldn't expect it, would you?"

"Shouldn't Derek be at school?"

"Off sick, isn't he? I dunno if he's sick or not, but he says he is and I got no time to take him to the doc. I mean, you said it was all right to bring him."

"Of course. But why can't his father take him to the doctor, if he isn't working?"

"Carl? That's a laugh. He'd more likely give him a good belting. Can't stick kids being a trouble, see. Now Rocky don't mind a bit, funny that, innit? I'd better get on with the vacuum."

She abandoned Carl and Rocky, and went to see Derek.

He was sitting on the floor three feet away from the TV, eating crisps and watching a cartoon. He was pale, but she saw no sign of bruises. She asked if he was all right, and he replied, "Yeah." His hand dipped into the crisp packet and conveyed some to his mouth while watching the screen. She asked what was happening, and he said an elephant had dropped out of the sky. She left him when the door bell rang.

"Must be somebody's birthday," Patty said, and put the wrapped flowers into her hands. Judith removed cellophane to reveal red roses, along with a card that said "Our fifteenth. Love, Victor." She looked in a dazed way at the fifteen red roses, and remembered it was their wedding anniversary. No doubt that was the reason for Victor's greater than usual jauntiness at breakfast, and for his remark about being sorry it was this evening. Instead of celebrating on their own, they were going to a Chamber of Commerce dinner in aid of some good cause or other. Back in the bedroom she found tears in her eyes. Nothing to cry about, she told the face in the glass, but then there was not much to celebrate either. Again she said aloud, without knowing what she meant except that the words seemed an assurance of her existence, "I am Judith, Judith alone." She made the telephone call she knew Victor would expect and said it was wonderful of him to remember when she had forgotten. Then she paid Patty, got out the Ford Fiesta and drove into town to have lunch with Debbie Hatter at Luigi's Bistro.

2

She sometimes wondered why she was so friendly with Debbie, and decided it was because she envied Debbie's readiness to say all and perhaps more than she meant, the casualness with which she had shrugged off the publicity a few years ago when her marriage to a local doctor had broken up. The doctor had left for London with the wife of a patient and Debbie, who had been conducting an affair with Johnny Hatter so publicly that the details were all over town, had become the wife of who she called the Mad Hatter within weeks of the divorce going through. In spite of rumours about his temper and her eye for anything in trousers, they had stayed married and seemed still to be on good terms.

And why did Debbie bother with her? Perhaps it was again the attraction of opposites, perhaps just that she liked an audience. In any case, Debbie was waiting at the table, a glass of sherry in front of her; small, dark, lively, and as always bursting with news. Johnny Hatter was a property developer and wanted to build on part of Burley Common, an area on the other side of Wyfleet. Apparently there was some question about this part of the Common having been given to the town fifty years ago to be used for the benefit and pleasure of the inhabitants, and objections were being made to building on it, on the ground that only a small minority of the people of Wyfleet would benefit from the erection of the group of executive type homes designed by Victor. Johnny, Debbie said, was fit to be tied and ready to justify his name as the Mad Hatter by beating Nethersole to a pulp. Who was Nethersole?

"Judith Lassiter, I do not believe my ears. Don't you take *any* interest in what goes on? Norman Nethersole is on the Council, Labour of course, always making trouble. Mostly nobody cares, but this time he's got half a dozen of these Keep England Green, Friends of the Earth, Save our Countryside groups all going on about it. For heaven's sake, Burley Common's pretty dismal anyway, and there'll still be plenty of it left. Hasn't Victor said anything about it? He's working with Johnny on the plans, at least you know that."

Judith said she knew, although in fact she didn't. Victor rarely talked about his work, and when he did she paid little attention. Perhaps Debbie sensed her lack of interest, for she stopped talking about Nethersole.

"I'm going to stuff myself with pasta today and the hell with my figure. What about you, my girl, you look down in the mouth. Tell all to little Debbie."

What was there to tell? The slight feeling of shame at having forgotten the anniversary? Apart from that, nothing tangible, nothing at all. She had no intention of telling Debbie she had been sending love letters to herself. Instead she asked, for some reason she couldn't have named, whether Debbie had ever wanted children. Her friend shook her head.

"I'm not the motherly type." Her sharp eyes looked at Judith. "Shouldn't have thought you were either." The words lay between question and statement.

"I don't know, I sometimes think I am. You see, I had two miscarriages. The second was at six months, a boy. After that I didn't want to go on, and I don't think Victor did either.

Perhaps we should have." She poked at her chicken salad, and asked inanely, "What do you think?"

"I think you need a man. An affair, something to shake you up, take you out of yourself. You're what, thirty-five?"

"Thirty-seven."

"You don't look it. I'm five years older, and every six months or so, I get the urge."

"What happens then?"

"That would be telling. But if I do something I make sure Johnny doesn't find out. He'd beat me black and blue." She contemplated the possibility for a moment. "I love this fettucini, I feel better already. Eating's a substitute for sex, they say. What about Victor?" Again her eyes were sharp. "What would he do?"

"I don't know." I am not like you, she wanted to say, what I desire is love, I want a man to tell me I am beautiful whether he thinks so or not. She had to restrain herself from a shudder at the crudeness of Debbie's comparison between eating and sex, as she had shuddered when touching herself. Just momentarily she felt a revulsion from her companion which Debbie, choosing a pudding from the menu, didn't notice and if she had noticed wouldn't have understood. A phrase came into her mind: roses were a substitute for love. She said, "We've been married fifteen years today. Victor sent me roses."

"Nice. I shall have the Sicilian Surprise. I can eat what I like, never put on an ounce, isn't it wonderful, all your metabolism they say." A little later, spoon dipped into the whipped cream depths of the Sicilian Surprise, she said, "So you're celebrating. A night in town, a show, then supper at the Savoy."

Judith gave the briefest laugh and said what they were doing that evening. Debbie, raising another spoonful of whipped cream to her mouth, said she and Johnny would be there.

"You've got to see and be seen, Johnny says. You're like me, you want a refresher course, that's what I'm taking."

17

A *refresher course*—she closed her eyes and saw herself clearly, wearing some highly coloured flowing robes, reclining on cushions, a handsome Arab kneeling before her and saying, "I worship you, at the well of beauty I am constantly refreshed." The picture and some of the words came from a TV chocolate advertisement, yet she was reluctant to open her eyes and abandon it. Debbie was saying something. *I could do it for you*—what was it Debbie could do for her, make the picture real? She opened her eyes. "What could you do?"

"Book it for you."

"What?"

"The refresher course. I knew you weren't listening. You know Ron's Motoring, they've started this refresher course for drivers who feel they're not up with all the new signs, all those red triangles and things that look like those shapes that are supposed to fit together but nobody except kids or old men can make sense of them. I mean, could you answer questions about what a triangle upside down means? You get practical things too, that stuff about reversing and three point turns we've all forgotten. And the thing is—" she pushed away the Sicilian Surprise and ran her tongue over her lips—"the one I've got is very dishy." Judith said she couldn't think why she should have to answer questions about the Highway Code, and Debbie shook her head, more in sorrow than irritation. "You're looking peaky, need taking out of yourself. I'm going to book a course for you, four lessons, it'll be a present from the Mad Hatters. A fifteenth anniversary present to go with the roses."

Again there was a phrase that stayed with her when she had parted from Debbie. She had left the Fiesta in the car park beside what had once been the Odeon but was now a supermarket, and was walking down the High Street to the charity shop where she worked three afternoons a week. You need taking out of yourself—she could see what was happening: some essential Judith emerging from the shell, placing one foot carefully in front of another on the pavements and moving

18

beside her, a Judith who trod more lightly and had a gleam in her eye that caused men's heads to turn. This Judith was clearly visible, walking ahead and a little to the left, and she was admiring it when somebody bumped into her so hard she almost fell, and a red-faced man wearing dark glasses and carrying a stick asked why she didn't look where she was going.

"You almost knocked me over."

"Me? She walks slap straight into me as though she can't see more than a couple of feet ahead, then says I knocked her over. Some people." Passers-by murmured agreement, one asked if he was all right. "No thanks to her. If I had a guide dog she'd have tried to tread on him." She said she was sorry, then stood looking into a sweetshop window. Behind her reflection there was no sign of the other Judith. I must stop this, she thought, there is no other Judith, I am Judith alone.

Mrs. Butterworth, Mrs. Chappell, Mrs. Bell, all the charity shop ladies greeted her with a warmth that made her feel as if she was sinking into cushions. Not that she sank into anything, there were piles of clothing to be sorted and priced, a collection of junk from pin-cushions and a set of miniature screwdrivers to a device for pushing nails into walls without using a hammer, dozens of things to be picked over in the hope of finding a jewel or two among the dross. But her particular usefullness lay in the fact that she had been trained as a typist and was able to use the ancient Underwood manual machine more quickly and efficiently than anybody else. She settled down to the mechanical business of making lists of things that had to be sent up to central headquarters in London because there was no sale for them in Wyfleet, writing letters to shops and businesses suggesting ways in which they could help the charity, typing the draft notice of a special sale they were having next month. Mrs. Bell, fat and fifty, wife of a local butcher, expressed amazement at the speed with which her fingers tapped the keys.

"I took a typing course. It's almost the only thing I'm any good at."

"Go on, I don't believe a word of that." Mrs. Bell settled comfortably into a chair beside her. "Somebody's been clearing out things after a lady passed away, there's a lot of old photos. I don't know what we can do with them, put them in the card bin I suppose, but some seem too good for that, you'd think the family would want to keep them but the gentleman who brought them in says no, it's his aunt by marriage who died and nobody's interested, it's all past and gone. I think it's a shame to get rid of things like that, don't you? I mean it's all history really, isn't it? Didn't you live at Cross Lanes once, would you like to have a look?"

She took the thick pack of cards and photographs and began to look through them. Most were cards signed Jack, Peter, Bill, Eleanor, saying thank you for this or that, writing of happy holidays, delayed trains, recovery from illness. They were destined, as Mrs. Bell said, for the card box where collectors might buy some of them, attracted by old views of towns and villages and seaside resorts, perhaps concerned with the written messages. Suddenly her attention was snagged by the hood of a recipient's name. Then she noticed the address, Eldred Cottage.

"Mrs. Noon," she said. "Emily Noon."

"The gentleman who brought them was called Stanford. Did you know the lady?"

"Mrs. Noon and her husband were friends of my mother and father." She said almost accusingly, "Most of these were sent to another address, not Eldred Cottage."

"That's right, dear. Mr. Stanford told me the lady, your friend that is, was in a nursing home her last few years. But you'd lost touch, I suppose."

She did not reply, but looked at the cards and photographs now with a strained attention. A little more than halfway through the pile was the card for which she had perhaps subconsciously been looking. The postmark was somewhere in Brittany, the card was addressed to Mr. and Mrs. Noon in a childish hand and read: "Having a nice time, swimming a lot, dad had to go back to London, good weather, love Judy." She was ten, everybody called her Judy, she had been happy. A year later the world ended. Nowadays she could not bear to be called anything but Judith.

She knew there was something more to be found, and it was there under the cards, among the photographs. A rather blurred picture, no doubt taken by Mr. Noon who was always getting the focus wrong, but the house was unmistakable and so were the figures. The photograph had been taken in the rose garden at Three Gables. There, in front of the dull red brick of the Victorian house and the six steps that led down from the terrace into the garden, stood her father and mother, he glaring at the camera beneath a panama hat, she with a hand raised to pat her hair in place. She separated this photograph and the postcard from the rest.

"This is my mother and father and our old home. And I wrote this card."

The vehemence of her tone disconcerted Mrs. Bell. "What a nice surprise. I expect you'd have liked to talk to Mr. Stanford."

"No. I never heard of him. I don't know how anybody could be so callous, throwing out things like that."

"People do it all the time. I mean, you can't expect them to have the same meaning for him as for you, can you? But of course you keep them, they belong to you."

"I don't want them. But I don't want anybody else to look at them either." She tore the postcard in half, the photograph into several pieces, and dropped them into the wastepaper basket beside her desk. Mrs. Bell nodded, gathered up the rest of the pile, and departed to the front of the shop where Mrs. Butterworth was selling a leather jacket to a young man. Judith returned to the Underwood.

3

Thoughts of the card and the photograph stayed with her through the rest of the afternoon and the early evening. They infiltrated the novel she tried to read, *Jennifer's Problems*, about a young woman (they were all young, the women in the novels she read) who parted from her husband because she was determined to carry on her career as a journalist, and didn't want children. She had an affair with someone working on her paper, tried to kill herself when he left her, and in the end returned to her husband, reconciled to giving up her job and starting a family. The words on the page were so much less real than the fairytale happiness of her life at Three Gables that she gave up reading halfway through, looked at the end, then put the book aside feeling it was rubbish. Life was not like that.

But then what *was* life like, or what should it be like? Not like a romantic novel, but also not like making breakfast for Victor, working at the charity shop, keeping Green Diamonds looking as Victor wished, shopping and cooking and devising menus for the dinner parties they gave for people with whom Victor was doing business or his colleagues from Group South-east. If that was life, what was the point of it? Mrs. Butter-worth had been very strong about the pleasure to be got from joining the Women's Institute or perhaps it was the Townswomen's Guild, but Judith did not want to sit around with a lot of other women discussing whether next month's talk should be given by somebody who had lived ten years in Borneo or a man who had discovered a way of making attrac-tive hats out of cardboard. It occurred to her sometimes to wonder what did interest her, and the only answer she could think of was the idea of love. Further back there was child-hood, Three Gables, her loving father and absent-minded charming mother, then laughing Uncle Puffin and Aunt Lilian with the red nose and Hubert, but these were things she tried to shut out of her memory.

Yet she accepted there was a pattern to the way she lived, and rules to be obeyed. When Victor came home she thanked him again for the roses, said again how stupid she had been to forget, and implied but did not say how wonderful he had been to remember. Victor was pleased, kissed her, said there was no need to dress up, it was after all only the Chamber of Commerce, and promised a celebratory dinner tomorrow night at the Grand, which had the most pretentious, although not the best, food in town. Victor was rarely in a bad mood—his cheerfulness had been one of the things that first attracted her—but this evening he had the exhilaration of manner and extreme brightness of eye that she recognized as marking the hope that he could pull off some contract about which he could boast to the Old Man when they saw him on Sunday. She had realized long ago that one of his chief objects in life was to win not just the approval but the admiration of the Old Man. Now, after he had bathed and put on what he would have called clean linen, although in fact neither his shirt nor his underclothes were linen, and donned (the only word for it) a different suit and another striped bow tie, he came into her bedroom, kissed her shoulder, and said, "You're beautiful, you know that?"

She was sitting at the dressing table, and was conscious that he was regarding himself rather than her in the glass. She said thank you, contemplated the long dark hair that framed her long face with its slightly too emphatic chin, and decided he was wrong. When he had approved the black dress and white collar she was wearing he said, "You saw Debbie at lunch, I expect she told you Johnny will be there. And that bloody MacGregor who edits the local rag, the Mayor of course, and Dick Casement, leader of the Council, both plus wives . . ."

She had heard similar litanies before, and gave him only half her attention.

". . . as I said, wheels within wheels."

"What was that?"

"A man named Nethersole and his wife Norah. He's an awkward customer, no need to bother with him, but you might try exercising your charms on Norah. I think she's having a rough time at the moment, could be pleased to find a sympathetic ear. No need to put yourself out though."

"You think if I give her a sympathetic ear she'll persuade him to change his mind about Burley Common?"

Victor's laugh was unconstrained. "Debbie's been talking. Nobody who knew Nethersole would think your chatting to his wife could make him change his mind about anything. It's just that being friendly to her might make him a mite more approachable, that's all."

The Wyfleet Chamber of Commerce dinner dance in aid of Ethiopian Famine Relief was held in an annex to the Town Hall. There were around a hundred and fifty people, most of the women wearing long dresses, most of the men in lounge suits. Johnny Hatter and Debbie were almost the first people they saw, he genial, burly, wearing a dinner jacket that looked too small for him, Debbie in what Judith thought an unwise bright red dress. In two minutes the men had joined a group at the bar in a way she knew to be customary at such functions. She found herself among a dozen women, half of whom she knew. Drinks were brought round, and she took a dry sherry. Debbie said, "I've fixed it." Judith looked blank. "Your refresher course. I told you at lunch. I said a present from the Mad Hatters."

"Very kind. I really don't need it."

"Take you out of yourself. I tell you, you'll enjoy it. And you won't be such a menace on the road. First lesson tomorrow, two o'clock, it's booked. I gave them your number, someone will ring in the morning to confirm."

She was about to say Debbie had no business making arrangements for her, then saw an expression of concern on her friend's face and was silenced. As if to confirm the expression Debbie said, "I worry about you, I really do." At the same time a voice said, "Mrs. Nethersole," and she saw Mrs. Butterworth from the charity shop talking to a thin-faced woman wearing a short blue dress, matching beads and blue-rimmed spectacles. A minute later Mrs. Butterworth had introduced them, and in another moment was nowhere to be seen. Mrs. Nethersole glared at Judith through the blue rims and said, "Disgusting." She expanded on the word. "Eating for charity. If they want to help poor people there are enough here in Wyfleet."

"I thought this was a prosperous town."

Mrs. Nethersole made a curious sound through her narrow nose, between a snore and a snort. "*They're* prosperous all right, the ones who come here. Pigs with their noses in the trough. You want to go down to the new estates, you'd see things there."

"As a matter of fact a girl from the Orchard Estate works for me." Too late she realized this was not something of which Mrs. Nethersole would approve. Too late also, she knew the lame addition "She's very nice" was not likely to help.

Sure enough, Mrs. Nethersole repeated with emphasis "*Works for you*," and gave the snore/snort again. Exercising

25

charm on her seemed an impossibility. Abandoning the attempt, she asked why Mrs. Nethersole was there, since she disapproved so strongly of the dinner's purpose.

"The first time. And the last. That's my husband, over there." She indicated a man as thin-faced as herself, who might have been her brother. "Norman thought—" She did not say what Norman thought, but added aggressively, "He's on the Council, thought I should come. Didn't catch your name, a little deaf."

Judith told her, and was aware of a change in her manner. It was no less aggressive, but seemed striving vainly for amiability as she said, "You're married to that architect."

"My husband's an architect, yes."

"Have you got children?" Before she could ask what business it was of her companion's, Norah Nethersole said surprisingly, "Shouldn't have asked, I'm sorry. We've just the one, Edgar, he's a fine boy. And clever too. Only he's run into a bit of trouble."

"I'm sorry."

"Your husband's the architect," Mrs. Nethersole repeated. "Thick as thieves with that Hatter, isn't he?" She said angrily, "*He* could do something." The gong sounded for dinner. Judith felt like a boxer reprieved by the bell.

At dinner she sat between Johnny Hatter and the Chairman of the Council, Dick Casement, who wore a dinner jacket too big for him and a dress shirt that was too small, so that he kept feeling his neck uneasily. Above it a little nose twitched like a rabbit's as he spoke of the wonderful weather they were having, and how awful the famine must be for the Ethiopians. When Judith repeated, without endorsing it, Mrs. Nethersole's remark about eating for charity his nose twitched alarmingly, he fingered his collar, and turned to his neighbour on the other side.

Johnny was much more talkative. He told her Victor had excelled himself in designing the Burley Common houses, five different types each absolutely individual yet blending perfectly with the surroundings and with each other. Then he asked suddenly if she knew MacGregor. Hardly at all, she replied. "You see that paper he runs?"

"The *Mercury*? No, we don't take it."

"He's running what I expect he calls a campaign against the Burley Common scheme. Seems to have got me specially in his sights, I don't know why. He's playing dirty, MacGregor." He grinned. "Doesn't know what he's up against. You know why I'm letting off steam to you?" She said no. "You're the soul of discretion, my beloved wife always tells me. Which is more than I can say for her. What's this stuff she's taken up now, something about refresher driving lessons, who wants them?" She said Debbie had arranged for her to take a course. "No harm in it, I suppose, though I don't trust Debbie, or any woman come to that. They all want watching. And keeping in line when they stray."

The accompanying grin was meant to show he was not serious, but she knew he was, or might be. Debbie's remark about being beaten black and blue was occasionally given visible substance by bruises to be seen on her arms, and a couple of years earlier an altercation about access to a car parking space with another motorist had ended with Johnny breaking the other man's jaw. He had the square compactness of a middle-weight boxer, and his blue eyes were both angry and unfocused as if he were staring at an invisible scene of violence, a stare that perhaps justified the name Mad Hatter.

He was, as he often said, a self-made man, his father was a local brewery hand who had lost his job and then drunk himself to death while Johnny's mother went out cleaning. Johnny did a newspaper round, got a job as a clerk to an insurance broker, borrowed and scraped together money to buy a bit of land which became valuable when a new road was planned to run through it, and never looked back. Women were said to find attractive his aggressive maleness, the dark hair sprouting on the backs of his hands and no doubt the rest of his body, and the fiery look that threatened or promised to become a blaze.

Victor was at another of the round tables, and at times she thought he was watching her. After dinner, when they danced together, she said he looked worried about what she might be saying.

"Why should I worry? Don't you know my wife has the reputation of never saying the wrong thing? I know you sometimes find Johnny a bit much, that's all."

"Perhaps. But it was nothing, he was just being Johnny Hatter. He said MacGregor was running some sort of campaign against him."

"In the local rag, yes. Nobody takes any notice. I saw you talking to Norah."

"I don't know how you thought anybody could charm her. She seemed interested in you."

"Showing taste. What did she say?"

"Mentioned you, then her son Edgar. What's it all about?"

He didn't answer, but asked what she thought Norah looked like. "A stork, do you think? Or one of those long-nosed animals, do I mean an ant-eater? Thanks, love, for talking to her. I'm going to brave the ant-eater."

He went up to Mrs. Nethersole who sat with arms folded, looking at the dancers with disapproval. Judith saw her shake her head decisively, then Victor take the chair beside her and begin talking animatedly. What could he want with her? She had no time to speculate because a stranger asked her to dance. She was so surprised that she said yes—but why should she have been surprised, or said no?

He was dark, wore a blue suit, had tiny tufts of hair on his cheeks, and was not so light on his feet as Victor. They had not been on the floor a minute when he said, "Tell me something, you're the most attractive woman in the room." His voice had a trace of the local burr, but with a workaday coarseness that might almost have been cultivated. She said his was an unoriginal approach.

"Sorry about that."

"And untrue. That blonde in the corner is ten years younger than me and five times prettier."

"Didn't say pretty, I said attractive." He held her away from him so that they looked at each other. She saw a hard face under thick hair growing low over the forehead, nose slightly hooked, the faded mark of a scar high on one cheek. "There's no comparison. She's pretty all right, but wood from the neck up."

"You know her?"

"I know everybody. Her name's Verne, Verne Upwood. She's a hostess at a club called the Red Dragon. The man you sat next to at dinner brought her."

"Johnny Hatter?"

"Other side, Casement, Council leader."

"She didn't sit next to him."

"Not possible, Mrs. Casement's here. Casement arranged for an ex-boyfriend of hers to bring her. Got an eye for the ladies has our Dick Casement, though you might not think it. Expensive ladies too. She's got looks, Verne, but she's thick as two planks. Otherwise why should she have wanted to come to this do?"

"Why do you know about her? Who are you?"

"The name's Jack Craxton. We know each other, or used to. Remember the school at Cross Lanes, old Mrs. Richards? You had fair hair, wore a pigtail. You wouldn't remember me, why should you? I was a year older, not too bright, snotty little kid. I liked you because you always looked happy. More than you do this evening."

"I don't remember. I mean, I don't remember you at school. I left Cross Lanes when I was ten."

"I know what happened. Can I have the next dance?"

"I don't think so. My husband is here."

"He won't mind. He's too busy trying to get this project he's in with Hatter off the ground to worry about your dancing partner."

"I see you do know everybody."

"I should do, lived here all my life. Anyway he'd know you're safe with me."

"Why should he think that?"

"I'm a policeman."

4

There were times, and that Saturday morning was one of them, when she felt content, perhaps even happy. Content to be married to a man almost always cheerful and good humoured (a man who remembered their fifteenth anniversary), content with Green Diamonds which was after all in its way a unique house and one envied by many of their acquaintances, content with life in Wyfleet and her place in it, even content with her appearance. On this morning after the Chamber of Commerce dinner dance, she woke with a sense of freedom, which after some moments of confusion she traced to its source, which was that she knew she had done now with books like *Jennifer's Problems* and *The Lord of Courtney Castle*. She felt no desire to read any more of them, and she knew she had done also with the stupid game of writing letters to herself from imaginary lovers.

She could not have said what had effected this transformation, it had simply occurred. When she consulted the looking glass her eyes were bright, her skin glowed, her whole body seemed a collection of nerve ends tingling with pleasure. I am

31

a lucky woman, she thought. If it had been possible to embrace the figure in the glass she would have done so.

At weekends they indulged themselves with cooked breakfast, and exhilaration stayed with her as she cooked bacon, tomatoes and fried bread, the bacon crisp as Victor liked it, the bread rich but dry. I have a handsome husband, she thought as Victor came in with his dancing step, kissed her, stepped out on the deck singing "Oh, what a beautiful morning." He came back shaking his head and smiling. "Isn't it something, that view. Weren't we clever to build just on this spot?"

"You were clever."

"I did it for you. No, that's not right, I built it here because it was where I wanted to build a house." He gave her what, even in her euphoria, she thought of as the I'll-be-candid-with-you look he kept for clients. "But it was for the two of us, without you it wouldn't exist."

He ate quickly, delicately, fingers holding knife and fork so lightly it seemed they might drop from his grasp. "A bore for you last night. I'm sorry."

"Wheels within wheels." He looked at her, puzzled. "That's what you told me yesterday. As a reason for going."

"Did I? True in a way. How did you get on with la Nethersole, not too well I gather. Never mind."

"She asked if I had children, then said she had a fine son but he'd run into a bit of trouble."

"She said that?" He pushed aside his plate. "Delicious. Perfectly cooked. Though it's the smell of bacon as much as the taste that's important. English smells quite different from Danish or Canadian."

"Victor, please. What is all this about, why did she ask if I was the wife of the architect, and then start talking about her son?"

He put a dab of butter at one side of his plate, a small spoonful of marmalade at the other, cut a piece of toast into quarters, spread butter and marmalade on one quarter. "Edgar is her darling. He's also very clever with computers. He works at Braden's."

Braden's was the biggest firm of building contractors in the town. Victor went on, "Edgar has a habit. And he's been naughty."

She knew a habit meant drugs, but what did he mean by naughty?

"Don't ask for the details, it's beyond me how you fiddle with computers, but he's been doing just that, adding imaginary items here and there and hoping they'll stay unnoticed. Done quite cleverly I understand, except that some other computer buff did notice, and Clive Braden learned what had been happening."

"So he's been sacked, and she wants you to help get him another job?"

"Not quite." He put butter and marmalade on another quarter of toast. "The question is, should Edgar be prosecuted."

Even though he raised an eyebrow delicately, humorously, after saying this, she did not understand. Clive Braden, who had come to control of the family firm via Winchester and Balliol, had exquisite manners and a voice even more clipped and strangulated than that of his wife Eleanor, who was the daughter of a retired major-general. On their one visit to Green Diamonds she had looked at the roof incredulously and said, "How very original." More relevant to Edgar's fate perhaps was Braden's reputation as the toughest employer in the Home Counties. She guessed again. "Braden wants to prosecute and you're trying to stop him."

"Still not it. If Burley Common comes off, Clive will be the principal contractor. Suppose Nasty Norman stopped beating his high moral purpose drum about this bit of land nobody ever noticed being sacred to the people of Wyfleet before he said so, the other bleeding hearts would soon lose interest. And if *that* happened Edgar Nethersole might be allowed to retire gracefully with a reference saying he was brilliant at his job but because of changes in the system being used it had been regretfully decided etcetera etcetera."

When she had digested this she said, "Blackmail."

"Not at all. Business."

"That's why you wanted me to talk to her? Why be so roundabout, why doesn't somebody talk to him?"

"You're putting it crudely. Nobody's talked to anybody. Nasty Norman had been made aware through Clive's chief accountant that the question of prosecuting his son is still under consideration, but that nobody wants to damage a promising career. He's also had a letter from Clive enclosing full details of the Burley Common scheme and inviting him to discuss any modification he might have in mind. He's not such a fool he can't link the two together."

"But he's said no?"

"He sent three lines saying there was nothing to discuss. Simon Pure Norman doesn't want the scheme modified, he wants it dropped, so that the young may frisk and gambol over every bit of the Common, and their elders be mugged if they're unwise enough to venture there after dark. But la Nethersole might be able to persuade him, which is why I wanted you to talk to her. I believe she's particularly upset by the idea of the inevitable newspaper publicity if Edgar got a suspended sentence, which would be quite likely." He finished the last quarter of toast.

She felt the cocoon of contentment breaking as she heard the story. She told him she thought the whole thing revolting and was disgusted he should have had anything to do with it, or induced her to play a minor part. Victor got up, walked to the window and stood looking out with his back to her. One of the things she both admired and regretted about him was that he never lost his temper. He did not do so now, but as he spoke in a voice higher than usual she realized he had come near to it.

"It amazes me that after all this time you still don't live in the real world, and hold up your hands in horror when you find out what happens in it. I told you this because you asked, but I should have known better. When contracts are signed palms have to be greased, when obstacles are put in the way of deals somebody gets hurt. The Nethersole boy has been stealing from his employers. Are you saying he shouldn't be punished? Perhaps you are, and if Nethersole gives way to what you call blackmail and I say is friendly persuasion, everybody will benefit. The boy will get another chance, and people in Wyfleet will get some houses which in architectural terms won't be a blot on the landscape and which nobody except a few cranks finds objectionable. As for your playing a part as you call it, all I did was ask you to talk to Nethersole's wife. I'm sorry if that damaged your tender morality, and I won't ask anything like it again."

The cocoon was broken, she was back in the world where she lived with a man from whom she sometimes seemed so far apart in feeling that they might be at opposite ends of the earth. She said something like that.

He turned from the window. "I don't understand."

"If we were at opposite ends of the earth we could talk on the telephone, and that might be better. Suppose you were in Japan and the Government there had accepted your design for a new Stock Exchange, and I was still sitting here, we could talk every day and never think about Clive Braden or Mrs. Nethersole."

Victor was never angry for long, and now he laughed. "I love it when you talk nonsense."

"But imagine it, just imagine it. Someone from Finland or Italy sees the Hillerman factory and commissions you to design something like it outside Helsinki or Rome." Victor's design of the Hillerman factory had been awarded an honourable mention in an architectural journal as one of the best buildings of the year, although that was several years ago.

"Wonderful idea."

"I'd come out to join you, we wouldn't be at opposite ends

of the earth any more. And there'd be no Bradens, no Nether-soles, no Chamber of Commerce. Then that would be reality, not this."

She felt his hands on her shoulders, his lips on hers. "You should have been the architect, not me. You'd have created something really original. But it's not reality, reality is grubbing around to get things done. I love what you're talking about, but it's fantasy."

"If you want it enough you can make fantasy come true." She finished her coffee. "Perhaps you don't want it enough. Anyway, I won't talk nonsense any more."

"I told you I love it, only I'm a humdrum person. Feet-on-the-ground Lassiter, that's me." He spread out his hands appealingly.

"Who's Jack Craxton?"

"A policeman. Detective Chief Inspector, I think, plain clothes. Why?"

"I talked to him last night. He said we were at school together when I lived at Cross Lanes. And that Casement, the man who looks like a rabbit, has an eye for the ladies. Is that true, do you think?"

"I've no idea. He's a good fellow, Dick Casement. Did Craxton say anything else about him?"

"Only that he'd brought some club hostess as his guest, though she didn't sit next to him. He seemed to know everybody."

"I think he does. He's supposed to be a tough nut."

"I rather liked him."

Victor made no comment on that, but said he had a meeting with Johnny Hatter and wouldn't be in to lunch. "And guess what we're going to talk about. You've heard of the Rolvo, Finnish rival to the Volvo? Turns out the Production Director of the company, Risto Karlsson, saw the Hillerman factory, was bowled over by it, wants to talk about designing a new plant just on the edge of town that would employ five hundred people. So you see fantasy and reality aren't always so far apart." He kissed her, was gone.

At eleven o'clock the telephone rang. A male voice, uncertain, said, "It's Billy Gay."

"Who? I don't know any Billy Gay."

"From Ron's. About the course."

"Oh yes, I'm sorry." She said inanely, "I didn't know the name."

"You've got an appointment, two o'clock, all right?" She said she supposed so. "Only I just got the number no address."

She gave him the address and spent a few minutes looking at the paper. Today it was *The Times*, because Victor hadn't taken it with him. The Israelis had shot seven Palestinians they said had been rioting. Somebody speaking on behalf of the medical profession predicted that half the hospitals in the country would be closed in ten years unless Government support was doubled immediately. An expert on global warming said it was now too late for anything but extreme measures to save two continents from starvation and advocated complete closure of the car industry in all countries. The stabbed Greek's Maltese girl friend had given evidence and said the Pole had nothing to do with the stabbing. In the hit man case the man Wimbly spoke to in the pub had gone into the box and agreed he had told Wimbly he might be interested in the proposition mentioned by the husband, whose name was Foster. They had met, and witness had told Foster he would be able to undertake the job he wanted done. Did you intend to undertake it? Council for the prosecution asked. Witness replied that he did not. He had immediately informed the police, and had been told to play along with Foster, and arrange a meeting at which he would be wired up. "Wired up?" the judge asked. The meaning of the phrase was explained to him.

She gave up the paper, closed her eyes, felt sun hot on her lids. The telephone rang again, and she felt sure it would be the young man cancelling the appointment. Instead she heard Debbie's eager voice saying she'd rung up for a natter, what a bore last night had been, there'd been no more than a couple of men worth looking at, and she'd danced with one of them but never got his name. Judith confirmed that he'd worn a blue suit and had tufts of hair on his cheeks and identified him.

"Oh my God. Johnny says he's bad news, nosy. If there's one thing I don't like it's a nosy copper, he says. Lucky he didn't notice us dancing cheek to cheek, he'd have beaten me to death." She trilled with laughter.

"Why should Johnny worry whether he's nosy? I liked him."

"So did I, darling, so did I. But you know Johnny's had his little run-ins with them, won't admit there's such a thing as a good copper. Except when they're stopping a demo, then he's all for them." Judith mentioned the course, said she must pay for it, and her friend's voice rose to a scream. "Darling *I won't hear of it*, it's a little cheer-you-up present, comes out of Johnny's account not mine if that makes you feel better, and he agreed with me absolutely you need taking out of yourself, told me you hardly said a word at dinner." Judith refrained from saying he had given her little chance. Debbie said *enjoy yourself*, and ended with what she called her dirty chuckle.

Debbie had raised her interest in Billy Gay, no doubt about it, and her first reaction at sight of him was that he looked disappointingly ordinary. He was a little taller than Victor, with blond hair that looked as if it had been blow dried, blue eyes, neat features and a round childish chin. He wore jeans, a T-shirt that said "Wherever it is I've been there" and trainers. His clothes and appearance were those of half the teenagers she saw in town. His voice too was a typical teenager voice, almost classless, with syllables enunciated yet run into each other with some letters elided, so that when he said, "Billy Gay, you've got a two o'clock appointment," it came out more like Billy Gay yougoa-twoclock-pointment. The car was a Nissan Sunny. He said she could drive her own if she liked, but she answered that she liked driving strange cars, got into the driver's seat and was about to start the engine when he said, "Hang on, there's stuff I'm s'posed to tell you. 'Bout the course."

As he talked about the usefulness of a refresher course in what was no doubt a spiel devised for him, and asked questions about the Highway Code some of which she was unable to answer, she found herself becoming physically aware of him in a way that made her understand Debbie's comment of *dishy*. There was something ingenuous in the looks he gave her as he talked about the course, and his apologetic smile when correcting her mistakes, that made him seem like a schoolboy. This impression of him as very young was enhanced by what she noticed were nails bitten right down on small and delicate hands. When he said, "That's it then, 'spect you're sick of hearing my voice, let's get on with it," the words were accompanied by a smile so charming that she felt she could listen to him forever in spite of the slovenly way he spoke. Instead she nodded, nodded again when he asked if she understood he would ask her to stop if he saw her doing something wrong, and then—her words seemed to come of their own volition—asked how old he was.

"Twenny-one. Bin driving since I was seventeen, doing jobs around cars the last coupla years, driven all sorts, don't worry, I know about cars."

"It wasn't that, just—you do look young."

"Spect that'll change soon. Got problems like anyone else, 'nough to make my hair turn grey overnight sometimes. Where d'you wanna go?"

The words came from somewhere other than her conscious mind. "Cross Lanes."

"Okay. Away you go."

She drove away from town, took the left hand fork she always avoided and then a right turn past the group of poplars her father had for some reason always called the Giraffes, down the twisting road known as Lead Hill, then through what had been fields bordered with hedges in her childhood but was now one large open field turned over to oilseed rape, the hedges bordering the road and those between fields gone, past a small rash of new houses, another right turn, and then she stopped looking and tried without success to remember the words of a poem about the roads you take in life, and her companion said, "Watch it," as another car appeared when they went round a bend on the grass verge and she said sorry and he remarked that the other guy needed his head examined. Then there was a long stretch past the mushroom farm, which had sprouted a growth of ramshackle low buildings and said it was J. Cooper, Farm Machinery and All Repairs, one more bend, and there was the meeting of the roads that gave Cross Lanes its name.

The house was there on the right and looked much as she remembered, the red brick, the gables, the dormer windows—solid, Victorian, permanent. There were the cottages, and down the right hand lane she glimpsed the farm where she had gone to get eggs, and had once dropped them all on the way back to the house. Down the left hand lane was the C of E school she had gone to when she was five, and apparently had known Jack Craxton. It was all as it had been, except for the petrol station at the confluence of the lanes on what had been open land. She stopped the car, sat staring at the house, then lowered her head almost to the steering wheel and wept. The boy beside her said Hey, what's up, no need to get upset, she was doing all right.

"It's nothing to do with driving. I used to live there, in that house, Three Gables. Until I was ten."

"Yeah, well, you remember things." But of course he had so little to remember.

"I was very happy. Then my mother and father died, quite suddenly, in an accident, and I had to leave. Just like that. It was awful."

She feared tears were coming again, then felt his arm round her and it seemed natural, almost inevitable to place her head

40

on his shoulder. She said she was sorry to be so stupid, she would be better in a moment, and this released a volley of speech as if she had pulled a verbal trigger, as he said no need to be sorry, he knew what it was like, at school kids said he was that way because of his name, he got into fights though he didn't like fighting, it ended up with his fighting a boy twice his size called the Tank, but he had been so mad he hadn't cared what happened. The Tank made his nose bleed, there was blood all over, but he had fought the Tank to a standstill and after that the others left him alone. By the time he finished she had stopped crying, wiped her face, and removed her head from his shoulder with a feeling of astonishment that it had ever been there.

"I'm afraid I don't understand. About your name."

"Gay, see."

"Oh yes. Boys can be cruel."

"It's life, you take it and you dish it out. But I'm not."

Again she was momentarily confused, until his laugh told her the meaning of the last words. She felt touched almost to the point of weeping again that this boy, with so little experience of the brutalities life can deal out, had tried to console her. Now he said, "You musta been here before, it's only a few miles from your place."

She said truthfully that she had always avoided it, but today felt suddenly she wanted to come back. He nodded.

"Yeah, best way to get rid of it, stuff worrying you." She thought but did not say she would never be rid of it. He smiled at her as he said they had better get on with what they were supposed to be doing. She was not bad, not bad at all, a good driver, just a few points she should bear in mind, things she did that were all right by him but not the way they were laid down in the Code. As he told her about hesitations on mini roundabouts and failure to change down on Lead Hill, and faulted her for not knowing the sign indicating a staggered junction, she nursed a feeling that beneath this conversation he was saying they shared secrets, she with her yearning for

an unattainable past, he with the persecution he had suffered
at school. Then they were back at Green Diamonds and he
said, "Heard about this place, din't know who lived here,
dead clever building it here, I like it. Your old man built it,
din he?"

"He designed it, yes. How did you hear of it?"

"You hear stuff around. I live on the Estate, not far away.
With my mum." The sideways glance from his blue eyes was
confiding. "Though I'm not staying for ever." When she asked
if he knew Patty he was vague. "Dunno, think I seen her at a
disco coupla times, like she's got friends are friends of mine,
know what I mean?" She didn't know, but said she did. When
they parted after arranging that the next session would be in
three days' time, on Tuesday, he touched her hand briefly,
smiled, then was off down the drive.

Victor had not returned. She undressed, lay on her bed and
thought about the idyll of Three Gables. Had it truly been
idyllic, or was that a child's invention? Her father went off
each morning to what her mother called something in the
City, to do with buying and selling of shares and the floating
of companies. Her mother never got nearer to an exact description, perhaps because she did not know herself or could
not be bothered to know. He came home every evening in
time to play with her and read a bedtime story after Nanny
had bathed her. Nanny had been with them ever since she
could remember, and was called that although she was really
a housekeeper rather than a nanny. She stayed on when Judith
went to school, because Mummy was, as she said, quite hopeless at looking after things. There were several things Mummy
admitted or even claimed to be hopeless about, among them
cooking and gardening and knowing how much things cost, so
it was fortunate they had a cook and a gardener.

What she was good at was talking to people at dinner parties
and arranging flowers and being nice to what she said afterwards were the boring business friends of Daddy's who came
down at weekends. And Mummy was always good tempered,

42

laughed it sometimes seemed at everything, where Daddy was serious and exploded at times with anger when bills came in, though never less than adoring of his only child. Perhaps Daddy's seriousness was natural, for he was, as she heard Nanny say, a self-made man, while Mummy came from a good county family. She somehow knew it would not be wise to ask about this, but it seemed natural that somebody who had made himself would be serious, worried perhaps about his various pieces falling apart at some time.

Certainly in her memory it was an idyll. In the summer, dinner parties and garden parties, in the winter, snow and sledding down the hill at the end of the garden, and Mummy's relatives coming for Christmas, though not Daddy's for he seemed to have no relatives. Had it really been like that? If she wished to she could remember complaints by Daddy about the way Mummy spent money, and by Mummy about Daddy being absurdly out of date over absolutely everything. For heaven's sake it's the sixties, Mummy said once, and from her other remarks about style and freedom and there being nothing you couldn't say or do nowadays, it was plain she considered him sweet but a bit of an old fogey. She didn't want to remember things, or the disagreements about where she would go when she left the little local school and began what Mummy called her proper education. Such things had been shut out of her mind for years, along with other memories like letters and photographs.

She preferred to remember, or perhaps to have created, the idyll that ended when Daddy flew to a business conference in Hamburg. Mummy decided she would go with him to look around and perhaps do a little shopping, and the private plane in which they flew crashed in the Channel. From the moment that Nanny, red-eyed, came to tell her the terrible news, her life changed. Mummy's brother Uncle Puffin came down with Aunt Lilian to take her away with them to their house in Islington, and she never returned to Three Gables. It was only gradually, over weeks and months, that she learned of the unsuccessful speculations Daddy had made so that there was no money, nothing but debts, and Three Gables and everything in it had to be sold, and she would now live forever with Uncle Puffin and Aunt Lilian. Of course it was not forever, but that was how it seemed to her at the age of ten. Many people remembered that year as the one when President Kennedy was assassinated, but she thought of it as the year when one life ended and another began.

5

Victor was at his best that evening, and could not be blamed for the failure of it. Yet perhaps it was partly his fault, because he should have told her he had invited the Hatters and the Bradens to join them for dinner. And he should have known she disliked Eleanor Braden, although perhaps he did know but had invited the Bradens just the same. In any case Judith was not pleased and showed it, interrupting Clive Braden when he was talking about the benefits the expected twenty percent increase in Wyfleet's population during the next five years would bring to the town. Who wanted it, she asked? Not the townspeople.

"I would never contradict a lady, especially one celebrating her wedding day," Clive said. "But the townspeople aren't always the best judges of what's good for a town. Did you ever know them in favour of pedestrian precincts? Yet once they've been made everybody loves them, including the tradesmen who said they'd be ruined."

"That's got nothing to do with it. And you needn't be so condescending, as if I were a child."

45

Smiling Clive apologized, but Eleanor said she hadn't known Mrs. Lassiter was an expert on town planning, and Johnny Hatter, who had drunk two large whiskies before dinner, said if they were going to be frank, what she'd said was bloody nonsense. Wyfleet was going to expand whether people like Judith approved or not, and the only question was if the expansion should be sensibly controlled or just piecemeal.

She said, "Does sensible control mean Edgar Nethersole's going to be prosecuted if the Burley Common scheme isn't approved?"

She regretted the words as soon as they were spoken. There was silence, then Victor clapped a hand to his head. "I quite forgot to say all shop talk is forbidden this evening. The party will now come to order and consider the serious question of whether we should have a palate-cleansing sorbet, Edwardian style, before the next course."

Johnny Hatter's face was very red. There was a snap, not much of a sound, hardly more than that of a clicking finger. Red wine stained the table cloth. Then, or a moment earlier before the wine glass was broken, he said distinctly, "Fucking hell." Eleanor looked away from the table, the corners of her mouth turned down. Victor said, "Johnny, did I understand you'd like the sorbet?" Then he laughed, Clive laughed, Debbie laughed, Judith found herself laughing too.

Back in Green Diamonds, the time near midnight, she said she was sorry. Victor again gave his easy laugh.

"Nothing to be sorry about. I should have told you about the Hatters and the Bradens, meant it to be a surprise. Thought you might be bored if we were on our own."

"Johnny was very angry. I shouldn't have said what I did."

"He'll get over it. Edgar Nethersole's the least of our problems." He did not say what the others were, but poured a whisky nightcap and asked if she would join him. Sensing his need for a prolongation of the evening she said yes.

"Fifteen years. I had my eye on you from the moment you

46

appeared in the office. A shy little girl." Hands clasped round knees Victor asked, "What did you think about me?"

"I thought you were handsome. And kind."

"The Old Man wanted to get rid of you, said you looked miserable."

"So I was."

"I should think so, being turned out by that old bitch of an aunt because you stayed out all night." That was what she had told him, and he had never questioned the unlikelihood of even Aunt Lilian being quite so Victorian. "And they never even put in an appearance at the wedding. Not that we cared, did we?"

Perhaps not, but the Old Man had cared, had conveyed to her without using the exact words how lucky a penniless orphan was to marry the son of a successful architect. Now she agreed with Victor that they hadn't cared. As if reading her thoughts he said she wouldn't mind seeing the Old Man tomorrow, would she, and she replied that it was more a question of whether he would mind seeing her. It was his son he wanted to see, she said, not his son's wife.

"Not true. He knows I married the woman who suits me best." She made no comment on this. Leaning forward, hands still clasped tightly round knees, he said, "I'll be glad if you didn't say anything tomorrow about Burley Common. I mean, like what you said tonight."

She couldn't resist asking if he feared the Old Man would call him a naughty boy. "What would it matter, you're not tied to his apron strings now? But don't worry, of course I won't say anything."

"It's simply I don't want to upset him, he wouldn't understand."

"I think he would. Understand, I mean. He might even approve."

"We shouldn't be arguing. Celebration day." He flung himself back in the chair, neat features sullen, mouth turned down

47

in pettish discontent. That's what you are, she thought, a son who always tried to please his father and now wants to please other people. She repeated that she was sorry and he brightened instantly, said it was not only celebration day but celebration night. For a moment she did not understand, then shook her head. Now he was on his feet, laughing. "Come *on*." She shook her head again. "Why *not*?"

"You remember last time."

"Weeks ago. What do you think—"

"What do I think the Old Man would say if he knew?"

"What do you think I feel? What a laugh it would give Johnny if he knew Victor's wife wouldn't go to bed with him."

"I said, did you remember the last time?" He shook his head, then averted it. She finished her whisky. "I'm going to bed."

He barred the way, gripped her bare arms tightly, tried to pull down her dress. When she resisted he bit her upper arm savagely, then her neck, and tugged more violently at the dress, so that it tore. The sound of rending fabric stopped him. He stood looking at her with astonishment for a moment, then said, "All right, bitch," turned and almost ran from her. His bedroom door closed.

In her own room she looked at what were already darkening marks on neck and arm. Love bites, she thought, if Johnny or more likely Debbie saw them they would think the celebration night had been truly passionate. She did not let herself think in details of the night a few weeks back that had been Victor's last attempt at lovemaking, but in the hour that passed before she fell asleep wondered if she had been at fault herself during their whole marriage. She decided that was probably so, but it was too late to change. She slept uneasily, dreaming she had been asked a question about the Highway Code by the Old Man, and that when she failed to answer he sneered and said he knew she was the wrong woman. The wrong woman, the wrong woman—the words kept echoing in the dream.

On the following morning Victor was less buoyant than

usual. In the afternoon, on the way to see the Old Man, he said, "You know he's very frail."

"So we should look like a devoted couple. I doubt if he'd care, but all right."

"As far as I'm concerned it's true."

"Yes, you send roses."

"Was that wrong?" She didn't answer. When he laughed, the easy laugh as if he hadn't a care in the world that had delighted her in the early days, she asked what was funny. "Just this squabbling about what they call in the courts marital rights, don't you think it's funny? The sort of stuff comics have been getting laughs out of for years. Suppose we were animals there'd be no problem."

"But we're not."

"True, O Wise One. I sometimes wish we were, life would be simpler." The conversation seemed, inexplicably, to have cheered him up, and he began to sing the theme song from his favourite film, *Casablanca*. " 'You must remember this, a kiss is just a kiss, a sigh is just a sigh.' " Was he laughing at her? When they reached the hospice he said, "Animals respect the old ones in the group or pack or whatever, and look after them, we've got that in common. Or should have."

They went to see the Old Man every Sunday, and Victor was insistent they should go together. The father-son relationship was close, one of dominance on the Old Man's part and what she felt to be slavish devotion on Victor's. When she worked in the office he had consulted the Old Man not only about every project but about every idea, and after he retired Victor rang him each morning with a report of how he planned to spend the business day. The retirement had come when, in a single year, his wife died from a coronary and his own tiredness was diagnosed as arising from a rare form of leukemia. A posse of specialists had agreed in giving him only a short time to live. That was five years ago, and although growing perceptibly weaker each year, he had proved them wrong. He had always taken pleasure in proving people wrong. The hospice was for terminal cases, but he had now been there several months. Judith sometimes thought he was immortal.

He was in bed reading the Sunday paper with the aid of a magnifying glass, the flesh gone from his cheeks, leaving only the thin promontory of a once powerful nose, arms like sticks with what seemed bones rather than fingers at the end of them, colouring chalk white. He put down the paper and said with a questioning, almost hostile note: "Well?"

Victor bent and kissed his father's forehead, Judith touched his cheek with her lips. It felt like rough paper. The *well*, she knew, meant the Old Man wanted an account of what had been happening in the firm during the week, the daily telephone call being long abandoned. She half-listened to what she felt sure was a much edited account of the firm's activities, then closed her eyes and saw Three Gables and her own small figure going down the lane to the village school and saying hello to, what was his name, Jack Craxton.

The Old Man's reedy voice asked, "Do you want the blind down?"

Victor stopped, momentarily confused. "What was that?"

"Sun's too much for Judith. Pull down the blind."

You old bastard, she thought, said aloud it was thoughtful of him, and pulled the blind halfway down herself. The Old Man showed a few yellow fangs. "Help you to stay awake. Order tea if you want it."

She left Victor explaining some details of a blueprint, found a nurse she knew, ordered tea, and asked about the Old Man.

"He's wonderful," Nurse Hill said. "You know he's weak as a baby. Doctor Walker says it's only will power that keeps him going. Half the day he's dozing, but I'm sure you found him bright and cheerful. He does look forward to seeing you both."

Not me, she thought, not the daughter-in-law who was never good enough for his son. She asked if Doctor Walker thought Mr. Lassiter had declined.

"Oh, he's just amazing. You know he should have—" She

stopped, started again. "Mostly patients who come here don't, how shall I put it, cling to life, they're ready to go. But Mr. Lassiter, he has such a will to live I don't think Doctor Walker would like to say. We all love him, he's such a character."

When she returned, the Old Man was lying back on his pillow, eyes closed. Victor, beside the bed, was staring at the floor. He looked up when she came in, his face tense with an emotion she could not fathom—worry, affection, love? He gathered together the blueprints and papers on the bed. The Old Man's eyes opened. They had always been deep-set, but now appeared to have sunk back further into his head. The little eyes, some indecipherable faded colour, looked from one to the other of them. The thin voice croaked something at her of which she heard only the words, "What is it?" She bent over the figure in the bed.

Now that she was close the croak faded to a whisper. "Something wrong," the whisper said. "What is it?" He had always been sensitive to anything troubling Victor. Was it possible he had discerned, without being told, the fiasco of their celebratory evening? He said something more, of which she heard only the word *money*.

Nurse Hill brought in a pot of tea, two cups, biscuits. The Old Man's eyes had closed again. Judith pointed at him, then at the cups. Nurse Hill shook her head, smiled, went out. She asked Victor softly, "What does he mean?" Victor shrugged. She poured the tea. The Old Man opened his eyes again and said quite clearly, "He's worried about money, didn't you know? You're his wife."

Worried about money? The thought had never occurred to her. She spoke to Victor. "You've not said anything."

"I keep telling Dad he's imagining things. I'm not worried about anything."

"Give me your hand, son." Victor obediently put his well-kept plump hand into the bony fingers. "I can feel it. Something. And the way you've been talking I know it's money."

"He's a wonder." Victor gave his easy laugh, then spoke to

51

his father. "Never say no to money. But it's a temporary cash flow problem, nothing serious."

"No money problems when I was there."

"I told you, when Burley's Common's gone through, the bank—"

"You took over a prosperous firm. No use looking to me for help." He said to Judith, "Either of you."

"Can you believe this?" Victor appealed to her. "I never mentioned the word money and, Dad, it isn't a problem. Believe me."

Pale lips formed the words "Cash flow." They drank their tea, ate the biscuits. The Old Man whispered something inaudible. Victor bent over the bed. "Won't be long now," the thin voice said. "You'll get it all then, do what you like. But I shan't bail you out, understand that." Victor made no reply, but drew back as if stung at the next words. "No good as an architect. No flair, no feeling. You tried, boy, I'll agree you tried." The eyelids drooped as if their weight was intolerable, then were drawn up again like shutters. "When I'm gone get a partner, if you can find one who knows what he's doing. Or sell the business. A pity not to keep it in the family, but no children. Never will be." The deepset eyes looked at her— did she imagine malevolence in their gaze?—then the shutters came down and were not raised again. Five minutes later they left.

On the way back she asked if it was true about money problems.

"Just what I said. Cash flow, an unexpected bad debt, interest rates gone up. And the bank is being awkward about extending the overdraft. Nothing to worry about."

"You should have told me."

"What would have been the point? Worrying you for no reason."

"He just guessed it?"

"Right, he's uncanny."

"It's not my fault there are no children. Or yours."

52

"Of course not."

After those two miscarriages in the first years of their marriage, she had what used to be called a nervous breakdown, and the doctor had advised against trying again.

On the rest of the drive home she wondered whether the Old Man's view of Victor's failings as an architect was right.

6

She found herself looking forward, not with eagerness but with expectation, to the second session in the refresher course, although she could not have said what she was expecting. Billy Gay wore what looked like the same jeans but a different T-shirt, this one saying "Take Care, Man At Work," and he looked even younger than before. When he asked if she wanted to go to Cross Lanes again she felt a jolt as if she had had a small electric shock. She said no, and they took one of the minor roads that wandered through the countryside towards the sea.

He told her to stop in a lay-by. "I better test you on the Code again, not driving, just stuff you're s'posed to know. You're on a side road like this, okay, no rain, brakes and tires okay, doing forty, what's your stopping distance? Feet or yards, don't matter."

"Forty's not very fast. Thirty yards?"

"Forty. Same conditions, but you're on the motorway doing the limit, seventy, what's the stopping distance?"

"I don't have much idea, I always seem able to pull up quickly if I have to. I'll say sixty yards."

"More than a hundred." He went on to details about over-taking, box junctions, giving way at roundabouts with what he called a two lane entrance, lane discipline on motorways, and she became confused, answering almost at random. Then he stopped, said she needn't look like that, she wouldn't need hardly any of this stuff. She asked if the course was successful.

"Not bad. Some partner of Ron's dreamed it up. Nine days' wonder, I reckon." A pause, then he went on. "Told you I had mates knew Patty, works for you, said she likes it, really does, know that? Some she works for are real cows, but she reckons you're different. Don't mind about her kid, that right? Some of 'em won't have a kid in the house." She felt absurdly flattered. "You know what, I reckon you've got something going for you too, or could have." She was aware of his hand placed at the back of her head, slowly turning it till she faced him. Then his face was close to hers, she closed her eyes, felt the pressure of his lips, the touch light and momentary as a butterfly's resting, no sooner felt than gone. "Sorry," he said, "just wanted to do it."

With what she felt even at the moment of speech to be absurd priggishness she said, "This is supposed to be a driving lesson," and restarted the car.

As she continued driving through the Sussex lanes, skirting towns and avoiding the direct route to the sea, she was aware of an ache in the stomach and an almost intolerable yearning for his touch. It was with difficulty that she restrained herself from taking a hand off the wheel and placing it on the nail-bitten hand that rested in his lap. When they were back in the drive of Green Diamonds she felt a tremor run through her body. She was waiting for him to speak, and he did.

"Told it's fantastic inside, your place. Any chance of having a look?"

She did not reply, but opened the front door. He followed

her in, exclaimed at the Bang and Olufsen TV and the electrically operated screen separating the dining area from the rest of the living room, then fell silent as she still said nothing. She took his hand, feeling again a thrill at the touch of his fingers, and led him along the corridor to her bedroom. There, before taking off her clothes, she spoke two words. "Be gentle." He was.

AFTERWARDS

It's a mess," Craxton said. "Lewis wants his brains tested."

Sergeant Ewbank felt it his duty to be defensive. "Fair's fair, he came up here, found this couple, only natural to think—"

"He should have been looking for one body, not two."

The scene of crime people and the photographers had been and gone, the area roped round, and a cursory search of the surroundings already made in hope of finding the weapon. Later on a more thorough examination was to prove more fruitful. What particularly annoyed Craxton was that the trampling of the grass made it impossible to tell whether the murder had taken place twenty feet off the road where the body had been found, or whether it had been done elsewhere and the body dragged there after being taken from a car. There were no signs of a struggle beside the shallow ditch where the victim had been found, but then they would have been obscured by intrusive feet. The police surgeon estimated the time of death as not less than twelve and not more than twenty-four hours before the body had been found by the factory worker, which, as Craxton said, meant he didn't take any risk of being wrong. Lover's Lane was not much used even in the daytime, but it was obviously more likely that the crime had been committed when it was dark or at least dusk, which on these June evenings meant not earlier than nine o'clock.

So Craxton reasoned, though he knew the reasoning might be faulty. He believed the murder had taken place somewhere else and the body dumped in Lover's Lane from a car or van, basing himself partly on the fact that the body looked as if it had been placed in the shallow ditch. If that was so, he said to Ewbank, it had apparently been important to the killer that discovery of the crime should be delayed. What did Ewbank think about that? Not much, would have been a candid reply. Instead the Sergeant said, "Bricks without straw," and Craxton replied sharply that it was their job to find the straw.

His first assumption about the murder having taken place under cover of darkness was soon proved wrong. After a post mortem the pathologist was able to narrow the time of death much more closely, to between 10 a.m. and 2 p.m. on the day before the body was found. It looked, then, as if the victim had been dumped from a car in broad daylight and then dragged over to the ditch. He took a chance and got away with it, Ewbank said cheerfully, and was told by his superior that the murderer had got away with nothing yet. The next move was to put out enquiries via posters, TV and radio, for anybody to come forward who had seen a car in Lover's Lane or any person behaving suspiciously there during the relevant times.

The special line set up was kept busy. Harrison Gant told his story to several papers but refused money for an exclusive, saying he was concerned only to show up a scandalous case of police neglect. He became a hero in his neighbourhood for a couple of days.

PART TWO

Something Like a
Love Affair

1

Memory is treacherous, as Judith sometimes said when she talked to herself, memory deceives and betrays and creates worlds that never existed, offers false pictures of the past to fill the vacant spaces of the present. All this she knew or believed, yet she still cherished the first years of marriage as a happy time, the time before Green Diamonds. They lived at number 27 Doyle Street, a little semi-detached house in town which had three bedrooms, one for guests and another for the baby, as Victor said. Victor had what often seemed crazily imaginative plans for private houses and public buildings that he would persuade clients to commission when the Old Man retired and he took over.

He complained, how he complained, about the Old Man's stinginess, lack of vision, rejection of any projects with an element of risk. And Victor had been buoyant then the whole time, buoyant and not merely cheerful and deliberately charming as he was now, but bubbling with the pleasures of being married and having his own house, his own even though the Old Man had put down the money for it. Their first wedding anniversary had been celebrated by dinner on their own with a flask of Chianti, not at the Grand with Johnny Hatter, Clive Braden and their wives.

That was all long ago, and perhaps memory betrayed her. Certainly there were things she did not want to remember, in particular the second miscarriage, the blood and the pain, the look of despair on Victor's face and the contempt she knew lay behind the Old Man's curt words of sympathy. It will pass, the doctor had said when she told him of the feeling of total emptiness she had afterwards, not only in her body but also as it seemed in her mind, so that she would forget what she was doing, leave food to burn in the oven, go out shopping and wander about unable to remember what she wanted and even where she lived.

That was what they called a nervous breakdown. She spent weeks in a convalescent home just outside Eastbourne. Victor came to see her every weekend and they walked in the several acres of grounds together, often hand in hand, he bursting with optimism as usual about ideas that might but almost never did take shape as buildings, and then telling her about the piece of land he had bought which had a marvellous view, and where he would build their new house. She could not remember how long she had been in the home, but she never went back to 27 Doyle Street. Victor carried her over the threshold of the just-completed Green Diamonds, exulted about the view, demonstrated the dividing wall and showed her the elaborate wardrobe fitments, the pipes run beneath the lawn for easy watering, the long American-style deck outside the living room, and the section of living room wall that moved back at the touch of another button to reveal a patio area paved with mosaic tiles and enclosed on all four sides for outdoor dining. And of course he showed her the shining green tiles of the roof. He had always hated living in a house with a number, Victor said, now they would have one known only by a name. He told her the name, and with an arm round her waist said, "Everything will be the same, nothing has changed."

The truth, she thought now, was that phrase reversed. Nothing is the same, everything has changed. But at times she was tormented by the fear that perhaps only she had changed.

The nervous breakdown had been, the several doctors she saw agreed, just that, a *nervous* breakdown with no physical cause. They agreed also on the importance for her of having what was called outside interests, something not connected with her husband or her home that would, in the phrase used by old Dr. Tufnell who had known her father and mother, take her out of herself. The phrase fastened on her imagination. If you were out of yourself where were you, she had once asked Victor? He laughed and said somewhere else, then that Dr. Tufnell thought it would be a good idea if she took up painting or sculpture or upholstery or cabinet making. There were evening classes at Wyfleet, and she was good with her hands.

So she had taken a course in painting, and produced daubs immensely inferior to Victor's watercolours done on holiday, things she refused to let him put up on the walls. She gave up upholstery after ruining a perfectly good sofa and abandoned drama because the lecturer upset her by looking like a younger edition of the Old Man. But she did feel the need of doing something that might make her forget the emptiness she associated with the loss of Stephen and Victoria, which were the names she gave to the things inside her that she had never seen as human beings. About all of this Victor had been, in the word everybody used now, supportive, although it was not exactly support she needed but something she was not able to define nor Victor to provide. He was kind, encouraging, cheerful, and she could not put a name to what was lacking. Or perhaps she did not wish to do so.

After the courses proved unsuccessful she had taken part-time jobs, in a dress shop, Wyfleet's bookshop that also sold stationery and offered photocopying and, later, fax services, and most recently in the charity shop. It was in her time at the bookshop that she had met Annabel Chambers, Wyfleet's novelist. Annabel was married to a history teacher at the town's comprehensive, and it was he who supplied the details of life in the eighteenth and early nineteenth centuries in which her historical romances were set. It was one of these, *The Heir of Malaway Grange*, that had started Judith on the many similar books she had devoured in the past twelve months as if (it occurred to her) she were a pregnant woman with a passion for a particular brand of chocolate. They had become friendly enough for Annabel and Percival to come to dinner two or three times, although Victor complained with justice that Annabel was unbearably gracious, and Percival talked as if he were talking to a class of not very bright students, whether the subject was politics, town planning, or the weather. And of course the novels had been partly responsible for those letters that now, the day after she had taken Billy Gay into her bedroom, seemed an unbelievable absurdity.

What she felt on the day after the encounter was a sense of lightness, as if she walked not on the ground, but a few inches above it. When she looked into the looking glass it surprised her to see Judith Lassiter's familiar features there instead of some different, more attractive face. She had no sensation of guilt, but an overwhelming need to talk to somebody about what she had done. Debbie? But Debbie would be unable to refrain from telling Johnny, from Johnny the word was likely to get to Victor, and she did not want Victor to be hurt. Annabel might be irritatingly gracious but she was also discreet. She rang Annabel, who as always said she was utterly immersed in her new book, but after making that clear accepted an invitation to tea.

This was one of Patty's mornings, and today it was Patty without Derek, who had pronounced himself fit for school. Rocky was away somewhere with his lorry, Carl in occupation, and Carl had said Mrs. Lassiter wouldn't have minded.

"I know, yeah, you been great, but he's right Carl, nobody wants a kid there all the time, do they? I mean Derek, I love him, but you got to admit kids are like, well, driving a car with the brake on, you can't do nothing you want to, go down the pub for the evening, have a bit of a laugh, know what I mean?"

They sat in the kitchen drinking instant coffee and eating chocolate biscuits. Judith asked if she couldn't leave Derek at home with somebody when she wanted to go out.

"If Rocky's there, yeah, but then Rocky wants to be down the pub doesn't he, I mean it's natural. He goes round to neighbours sometimes, but you never know, they could go out and leave two or three kids on their own. Never know what they might do then, burn the house down could be."

"Driving a car with the brake on." Judith laughed. "I've been taking what's called a refresher course in driving. I didn't drive with the brake on, but it turned out I wasn't up to date on the Highway Code."

"Who is? Lot of nonsense, ask me. Either you can do it or you can't Rocky says."

"My driver lives on the Estate, his name's Billy Gay. I wonder if you know him."

"Heard of him, don't know him. Goes around a bit with Carl. 'Spect I've seen him, don't know him, know what I mean?"

"He lives with this mother. He's a very good driver."

"Is that right? Should be, giving lessons."

She checked herself from saying anything more about Billy Gay and settled down to read the morning paper on the deck. Something called the intifada was going on in the Middle East. Israeli soldiers had repressed what they called a riot, four Arabs had been killed and an unknown number injured, including women and children. Was the riot an intifada? She could not remember. On the inside pages there was a story about a machine able to detect thought processes through electrodes attached to the head, and then print them out as machine-readable symbols. What was the point of that, a reporter asked? The scientist in charge of the experiment said it would help to analyze people who seemed normal but in fact had anti-social or self-destructive impulses. The article did not explain why, if they seemed normal, they would be prepared to have electrodes attached to their heads.

There was a column about the Foster case. Foster had struck unlucky with the man approached by Wimbly. He was a petty crook named Bert Williams, known as Doorlock because his speciality was stealing from cars, and he claimed to be able to get into any car in less than half a minute. Doorlock, however, made a little money on the side as a police snout, and it was in that capacity he had passed on the information about Foster. He had been nervous at the meeting with Foster and had managed somehow to unhitch his wiring, so that nothing was recorded. Hence much of the case was dependent on Doorlock's evidence about what Foster had said about teaching his wife a lesson, which Doorlock understood to mean killing her. Foster's counsel gave Doorlock a very bad time in cross-examination, suggesting that nobody should be convicted of anything on the evidence of such a witness. Foster in the box agreed he had said both to Wimbly and to Doorlock that he wanted his wife taught a lesson, by which he meant he wanted her frightened, nothing more. His counsel made as delicately as possible the point that a hundred pounds would be a very inadequate sum to pay for a murder. Judith wondered if Foster might be a case for the electrodes. She gave up the paper when Patty had gone, and baked a cake for Annabel to eat at tea.

Annabel was tall, with an intelligent horse face. She always wore dangling earrings, which today were jet black. She was a good listener, but although Judith had meant to talk about the afternoon she felt had changed her life, she found a reluctance to enter into an account of what had actually happened. It was her feelings she wanted to convey, not her actions. However, it was not Annabel's way to be impatient, and she approached Judith's adultery in the spirit of a surgeon probing before deciding how deep to cut.

"Delicious cake," she said. "This has happened only once? And do you intend to go on with it?"

"I'm not sure. But yes, I suppose so."

"It's like a situation in *The Heartbreak Heiress*, where Ester after a tumultuous night of love has to decide between her faithful, adoring but rather dull husband and the handsome lover she knows to be absolutely feckless. She feels she can't give him up, but knows she must though it breaks her heart." She brushed a crumb from her upper lip. "He dies at Waterloo."

"It isn't like that."

"That's what you feel. But it is. Ester gave up her lover. And so must you."

"It isn't—it's not right to think of him as my lover. He's much younger than I am. Perhaps to him it meant nothing at all."

"I understand, believe me I do understand. And sympathize." Annabel's bony hand tapped Judith's knee, and her tone changed from the coolness of a detached observer to the warmth of a fellow sufferer. "My dear, we've all been through the mill. I could tell you tales. But in the end I thought about Percival, and you must think of Victor. Everything's all right between you two?"

"I suppose so."

"You don't sound very sure."

"It's just that—I don't know." She found she could not talk about that attempt at violent lovemaking. "Perhaps we're not suited."

"After being married for years? Really, Judith." She paused, apparently on the brink of some decisive remark. "Can I have another piece of cake? I know it's dreadful for the figure." Annabel's figure was of lamp-post thinness. "How do you make it so light?"

"Make—oh, the cake. I could give you the recipe."

The earrings shook. "I wish I had the time. This young man—*much* younger than you, you said—my dear, you mustn't go on with it. A middle-aged woman and a very young man, what can it mean but heartache for the woman in the end? I don't want to know who it is"—she held up her hand, although Judith had no intention of telling her—"but what I do say is that Wyfleet's not a big town and these things can't be kept secret for long. Is that what you want, for people to gossip about you having an affair, making nasty little jokes behind your back? And what will you do when Victor gets to hear of it, as believe me he will? More important, what will Victor do? He's a good man, Victor, a good and I'm sure faithful husband." The earrings shook again. "I speak as your friend when I say you must make a clean break. Do it now. The longer it goes on the harder it will be."

How could she have thought it would be a good idea to talk about her feelings to a woman who half the time talked like an agony aunt, and the rest like a writer treating her as a character in a romantic novel? But what reaction would have satisfied her? Nothing less than a loving and understanding response, one that recognised a whole area of her psyche was left unsatisfied, desolate indeed, by life with Victor. Whether or not Debbie's stories of her affairs were true, they were not like hers, just what Debbie would probably call a quick in-and-out, or a one night stand. Did Billy Gay think about her in that way, had it been for him just a quick in-and-out, something he had forgotten in half an hour and would not want to repeat? That was a possibility she refused to contemplate. Yet it must have been in her mind, for when the bell rang a couple of days after that useless tea with Annabel, rang precisely at the time appointed, her heart began to beat more quickly and she sat, as it seemed immovable, on a chair in the living room, shivering a little in the summer warmth. When the bell rang again she pushed herself up out of the chair and walked on rubber legs to the door.

"Hello," he said. "Beginning to think I'd got the wrong day, you was out."

At sight of him she felt faint again but managed to say it was the right day, she was sorry to have kept him waiting.

"Don't matter," he said, then with a mock salute: "Your carriage awaits."

She tried to speak but failed, took his hand, led him to her room. Afterwards she thought she could not have borne it if he had made some coarse remark of the sort Debbie would have invited, said something facetious or knowing, or told her he'd been looking forward to this. She felt it to be a mark of natural tact and grace that he did not speak, but allowed her to lead him to the bedroom and there began to unbutton her shirt and unzip her skirt before removing his own clothes, all the while without speaking. Again he was gentle, she closed her eyes and was reminded of cousin Hubert, closed her eyes and cried out with pleasure as she came to orgasm as she never had with Victor. Afterwards he asked her permission before lighting a cigarette, something that again seemed to her a mark of natural tact, then sat propped on an elbow looking at her, smiling a little. His skin was very white. Then he did speak.

"Not done this before, have you?" She said no, and that of course he had. "I've been around." She said she understood that. "Reason I asked, I'd like to see you again, know what I mean? You're fantastic. But this, this here's not a good idea. I mean, what about your old man?" Faintly, in a voice she did not recognize, she said he was never back before six. "Yeah, but s'pose he did come back? I can look after myself, but, well, living up here's not like on the Estate, is it?" In the same faint voice she asked if he meant he did not want to see her again. He leant over, kissed her shoulder. "Course it doesn't. I've got the hots for you, thought you knew that. Look, all I mean is we oughta meet some other place. I mean, leave your old man out, you got neighbours, someone'll see my Sunny outside, think what's going on? Should be somewhere nobody notices, nobody worries." She asked if he meant a hotel. "Could be. I tell you, being here makes me nervous. For you, not me. Being with you means something to me, know that?"

"It does?"

"Not the sex bit, though—" He put his hand on her thigh. She trembled. "—that's fantastic. I mean, I got no intention of driving for Ron all my life or doing odd jobs and that. I want to do something, know what I mean? I know the way I talk's no help, lots of stuff you could teach me, I'd like that."

The words delighted her, with the implication that she would see him often, it was not just a quick in-and-out. She did not demur when he said it didn't make sense to leave the Nissan Sunny standing outside the house the whole afternoon, they should fill in some time on the refresher course, perhaps look for a hotel where they could meet. As she dressed, got into the car and drove off, and paid superficial attention to what he said about her driving, she thought again that the thing Annabel did not understand had happened, the whole nature of her life had changed. For the first time in years it seemed to have a meaning. That afternoon they stopped at three hotels, all several miles away from Wyfleet. She went in, leaving Billy in the car, found that two of them had rooms vacant for the day of the fourth and last session of the course, and booked a room in one of them. It was not the most expensive of the hotels but one called the Marvin in a small street on the edge of a town a dozen miles from Wyfleet. There was a smell that seemed to blend fried onions and disinfectant, the carpet in the hall was worn, she had to bang hard on a bell before a stooped ancient wearing an obvious toupee appeared from the back of the reception desk and said there would be a room free any time she wanted, no problem. "Out of season," he said. "Not much doing out of season."

So three days later Billy came to Green Diamonds, she got in the car and drove straight to the Marvin. It was she who signed the register using the traditional name of Smith, she who led the way up the stairs to the first floor room with the fruit patterned wallpaper peeling away with damp in one corner, the damp stain on the ceiling, and the dingy brown curtains matching the carpet which was not just frayed but had actual holes in two or three places. She did not like it, but it was not Green Diamonds and she forgave the room everything for that. She cried out again with pleasure at the act, yet when she thought about it afterwards it was not the act she remembered but Billy's gentleness that brought back again the memory of Hubert, and their long casual talk afterwards in which she felt nothing was held back, anything could be said. She had never known such freedom with Victor, not even in their earliest, happiest days.

There was a moment in that first afternoon at the Marvin when she felt revulsion. It was not from Billy but from herself, at her readiness to go to bed with this unknown boy. She asked him why he went to bed with her when she was old enough to be his mother.

"Ah come on, you should see my mother. Reckon you could give her twenty years." He saw she was serious. "Told you I fancied you, all right? It was mutual."

She knew it would be stupid to say he might not go on fancying her. Instead she asked about his mother and whether his father was still alive.

"Alive all right, the bastard. Don't live with us any more, though. Used to beat on me when I was a kid, and on my mum when she tried to stop him. He's big, see, and when he's had a few he gets stroppy like. I tried to fight him but that just made it worse, he took to beating Mum when I wasn't there. End of it was I got a couple of mates and the three of us got him in an alley outside one of the pubs he uses and gave him a going over, put him in hospital. After that he left me and Mum alone, then moved in with some woman he was going with. Court says he oughta pay maintenance, but does the sod do it? Not if he can help it."

71

It was the first time she had heard him speak with emotion. "You could do that, have your father beaten up?"

"No problem at all, do it again, you don't understand." He gave her his shy smile. "Sorry, but that's the way it is, he's just a bastard."

"You said you were going to be something. What sort of thing?"

"I dunno. At school I was, you know, pretty bright or so they said, but I could never get interested. There was some stuff I coulda been interested in, computers and math and that, but most of it was dead boring." He took out a cigarette. "You mind?" He lighted up. "I truanted."

"Much?"

"Fair amount. Do it again too, if I was bored like that. What I want to do, well, you read stuff in the papers about kids making fortunes in the market, just buying and selling, making phone calls, only numbers, I was always quick with numbers, reckon I could do it if I had the chance. They say getting the first twenty thousand is the trick, after that the banks fall over themselves to lend you money." He laughed. "Fat chance."

"The truanting. Was that why your father beat you?"

"And other stuff." He gave her a sideways look, at once cunning and innocent. "I got a record."

She found she was not surprised. "What for?"

"Coupla things, not much really. Borrowed a mate's car, only he didn't know it, then crashed it. Not my fault, swerved to avoid a kid running across the road, ran into a wall. Car was a write-off."

"If it wasn't your fault—"

"No license, see. Then I got done for B and E, breaking and entering, just bad luck. I was keeping watch outside, shouldn't a done it I know, got talked into it. I did six months. That was three years ago, swore I'd never go back inside and I never will." With an air of conscious virtue she found absurdly touching he said, "Took evening courses in engineering and that, I'm good with cars, you seen that." He gave her a shy

smile. "Not right that, is it? I shoulda said *you've* seen that."
He laughed, and she laughed with him, then he reached for
her again. "I'm ready if you are." Afterwards he said, not
bitterly but with a flat lack of emotion, "Doesn't sound good,
stuff I told you, does it?"

"I'm glad you did tell me."

"You've got no idea what it's like, none at all. That house
we stopped at, you were crying because you were happy. I
told you I understood, about fights I had at school, but this
stuff I been—I've been—saying, you don't understand it,
couldn't."

She said there were other sorts of unhappiness, other reasons for it. He said yeah, but she could see he didn't believe
her. But a week later, when they were again at the Marvin,
in the same room, the room of which the toupeed ancient
handed her the key without raising an eyebrow at their lack
of luggage, he said again in his own inadequate language that
those who'd lived from childhood sheltered from poverty and
brought up by loving parents couldn't understand what it was
like not to know at the end of the week if your mother would
have money to go out shopping or whether your father would
come home having lost most of his week's money gambling
and spent the rest on drink, and loosen his belt as he came in
the door ready to take out his frustration on wife and son. It
was then that, by way of proving that adolescence could have
other and perhaps worse miseries, she told him about Uncle
Puffin, Aunt Lilian and cousin Hubert.

73

2

In talking to Billy she said nothing about what she believed to have been the idyll of her childhood. Certain images of those years came back to her in any moments of reflection, particularly those associated with her father. There he was, a shortish ruddy man always going off in the morning to catch the train and do something in the City. She thought of the City as a place quite separate from London, which she had visited at Christmas to see the lights in the streets, go to a pantomime, and once or twice to stay with friends of Mother's who lived in a big house at St. John's Wood. She had been disappointed in London—there was, for example, no sign of the wood she had expected in St. John's Wood—and she did not associate those visits with the City because she knew a city had walls. He went away in the morning and came home in the evening, sometimes to spend half an hour with her in the playroom where a complicated train layout had been set up, and always to read her a bedtime story. She did not much like playing with the trains but pretended to do so because she knew even then that he enjoyed it, and she loved the

74

bedtime stories. Daddy was untidy and sweated a lot, Mummy looked cool on the hottest day and was always, as Daddy sometimes said proudly, perfectly turned out. Had they loved each other? For a long time after the idyll was over she thought so because she never heard them exchange a single cross word, but then it occurred to her that the same might be said of Victor and herself, and she was increasingly unsure that she loved Victor.

For a while, even when she had gone to Uncle Puffin's tall narrow cold house in Islington she did not really believe her father and mother would not come back. They appeared to her in dreams, her father saying he would soon come up and read to her, her mother laughing as she picked flowers in the garden, saying they must arrange a dinner party. She woke from such dreams not crying, but expecting that next day or next week she would learn it had all been a mistake, Daddy and Mummy were outside in the car and had come to fetch her home. It seemed to her that if she had the train layout it would make their return more certain, and one day she asked Uncle Puffin where it was, and if she could have it. He stared at her.

"Why, it was sold I suppose, along with everything else. It all had to be done in rather a hurry, you know. Were you specially fond of it? If you were, maybe at Christmas . . ."

Perhaps that was the day she fully realized, absurdly through the train layout, that the past was done with and her mother and father were never coming back.

Uncle Puffin was Mummy's brother. There was another brother and sister, and Judith learned afterwards that there had been a good deal of discussion about who should take the orphan. Really, though, it was inevitable that it should be Uncle Puffin, who had a job in the Ministry of Trade as an Under-something who became a Principal, or perhaps it was the other way round. In any case, the others were really not candidates. Brother Cecil had farmed unsuccessfully in three different counties, and was now running a mushroom farm in

Hampshire, and Mummy's sister Ellen had married a man who ran a clothes mail order business which was foundering because the goods were always being sent back by customers who complained of missing buttonholes, badly stitched shirts and blouses, and raincoats with removable linings that didn't fit. Brother Cecil or sister Ellen would happily have taken little Judith Bates if some cash provision had come along with her, but both had young families and the idea of another mouth to feed, another body to clothe, another mind to educate, had no appeal. Perhaps Uncle Puffin and Aunt Lilian, or at any rate Aunt Lilian, put up a fight, but the result was inevitable. She went to the house in Islington.

It was a narrow house in a narrow street. From the front windows you looked out at other houses, from the back on a tiny paved town garden with a vine and some plants and pots, a metal table and two chairs. Judith was a literal, foolish child. After two or three days, she asked Aunt Lilian why they didn't have a garden, and when told that the paved place with the table and chairs was the garden, said it couldn't be because there was no grass. Aunt Lilian repeated, "That is the garden," and then said, "We're not all made of money, you know, as your father thought he was." That evening she heard Aunt Lilian telling Uncle Puffin what she had said, adding that she was really a very stupid little girl.

"Hold on now," Uncle Puffin said. "Just a minute. Remember she's had a terrible shock, Eddie and Pam dying like that."

"You know what I thought of Eddie Bates. He was a chancer." Uncle Puffin made an indeterminate noise. "Just a chancer, didn't I always say so." Another indeterminate sound. "And who has to suffer for it? We do."

"Hold on there, steady now. It's little Judy who suffers most."

"Are you taking her side against me, telling me I'm wrong?"

"Of course not, my dear. Give the girl time, that's all I'm saying."

Uncle Puffin, whose name was really Peter, was kind but

weak. Everything about him lacked force. A few strands of thin fair hair were plastered down over his scalp, he had a little blond moustache that drooped because it lacked energy to stay level, his long thin head swayed uncertainly on a stalk-like neck, his clothes hung on rather than fitting him. His voice was reedy and rather high. It often began with the promise of liveliness, but lost power after a sentence or two and occasionally faded away altogether, ending in a series of puffing sounds responsible for his nickname. Yet Uncle Puffin meant well, as she even then realized. He was kindly, and on occasion generous, once giving her a ten pound note with a warning not to let Aunt Lilian know about it. He had come up to her top floor room, found her looking out of the window at the houses opposite, asked what was the matter, and she had broken into tears. Uncle Puffin was embarrassed and distressed.

"Here now, what's the matter? No need for that, you know, no need at all. Handkerchief?" He produced a handkerchief, she dabbed at her eyes. "Don't know what . . ." He left the sentence unfinished. "Not much fun here, but you have to remember . . . what's the matter then?" She said truthfully that she didn't know. "Life's not all beer and skittles, never was. Not for any of us. Remember that." She nodded. "Your aunt, you see . . . take this, buy yourself something, cheer up."

She cried out with astonishment. She had never had so much money in her life. Uncle Puffin began to laugh. "Know what? Thought that was a fiver, turned out to be ten. Your lucky day." He put a finger to his lips. "Mum's the word."

She did not have to ask what he meant. She was twelve years old, had five shillings a week pocket money, and if she bought anything that cost more than a pound or so Aunt Lilian would want to know where the money came from. In the end, she took a girl from her school named Hilda to see Laurence Olivier in *Love for Love* at the National Theatre. There was enough to pay for their gallery seats and a hamburger. Hilda was mad about Olivier and so was she, but he played Tittle, and they were both rather disappointed. She told Aunt Lilian Hilda's parents had paid for them. Uncle Puffin gave her a conspiratorial wink.

Aunt Lilian was a small woman with a sharp red nose. The nose was a curiosity, or at least the redness of it was, because the rest of her face was chalk white. The nose was perfectly shaped, thin and very narrow so that Judith wondered sometimes how she could breathe through those almost invisible nostrils, and the tip was redder than the rest. She had dark hair tightly pulled back, a buttoned-up mouth and a small pointed chin. Her father had been a Congregationalist Minister and Aunt Lilian went to chapel every Sunday, taking Judith with her as a matter of course. At Three Gables the family went to church only at Christmas, Easter and Harvest Festival, her father saying there were more good Christians outside churches than in them, and her mother being concerned chiefly with wearing clothes that might impress people she knew like their near neighbours the Noons. Mr. Noon was a retired bank manager who had the greatest admiration for what he called "the go" of his friend Mr. Bates, and untidy Mrs. Noon said how she admired Mrs. Bates' dress sense. In retrospect Judith realized that the Noons' worshipful feelings were the reason why they were welcome at Three Gables, and why she mistakenly thought they were Mummy and Daddy's best friends.

Aunt Lilian was a great disapprover. She disapproved of the Government, no matter what its political complexion, and also of the fact that the price of everything rose continually. She disapproved of a succession of women who came to help in the house, stigmatizing them as variously sly, dirty and sluttish. She disapproved of dustmen, postmen and the telephone service because they were inefficient, and when she spent three days in hospital for the removal of a cyst was outraged by the casualness of the doctors, the failure of ward sisters to assert their authority and the fact that two nurses called her "dear." She disapproved of Uncle Puffin because he had not risen higher in the Civil Service hierarchy, and of Judith because she was a financial burden as well as being lazy, ignorant and having learned nothing at what she said must have been a school for backward children. Uncle Puffin's insistence that Judith should be sent to a grammar school that involved a bus ride instead of the state school nearby caused her to issue constant reminders that money was being spent and, as she hinted, wasted, and to complain about the cost of school uniforms, sports clothes, and indeed clothing of all kinds. She spoke of Judith often in the third person rather as if she were a stray cat given a home out of mistaken generosity, and implied without actually saying that the expense of her school fees, clothing and food would bring the household to ruin. Aunt Lilian, then, was a disapprover. Her approval was reserved for her son Hubert. He was Uncle Puffin's son too of course, although Aunt Lilian referred to him always as *my son*.

She caused her niece great misery. No doubt the loss of her parents and the transition from Three Gables to the Islington house would in any case have made her unhappy, but Aunt Lilian's badgering made the unhappiness permanent. She would have been surprised to know this, for badgering came naturally to her and was always carried out for the badgeree's good, but the effect on Judith was to make her feel both useless and unwanted. She had few friends at school, in part because the volleys of criticism fired at the appearance and behaviour of any girl asked to tea after they had gone home, upset her so much that she did not invite them again. "What a silly giggling little miss . . . she ate and drank like a coster-woman's daughter . . . the way she flounced about and flaunted herself was really indecent . . ." The sharp red nose quivered a little, a sure sign of disapproval.

It was only the presence of cousin Hubert that made life at Islington at all bearable. He was in his very early twenties and looked like a younger version of Uncle Puffin, with the same silky fair hair but more of it, the same thin head, stalky neck and drooping moustache, the same loose-limbed, slightly shambling walk. His voice was soft, gentle, not yet reedy, and he had a smiling good humour that seemed to Judith to light up the whole house. In youth Uncle Puffin had spent some time in India and there had become an admirer of small wooden boxes, intricately carved and inlaid with mother-of-pearl or tiny semi-precious stones. He bought more boxes when he saw any with a novel pattern or form of inlay, and Hubert could be relied on to admire them. "I say, that's pretty *nice*," he would say of some box hardly distinguishable from several others. "That's a real addition to the collection, Dad, a proper corker."

When she was thirteen, Judith painted a picture in art class of Three Gables as she remembered it, which was said by the teacher to show promise, although in view of the disastrous failure of her painting course the teacher must have been mistaken. It was framed, an expense to which Aunt Lilian made no objection, perhaps because Hubert had expressed admiration for it, and hung in her bedroom. It was the Three Gables painting that prompted Hubert to suggest taking her to an Impressionist exhibition at the Royal Academy. They had lunch at Fortnum's, which she enjoyed as much for the place as the food, and at the show Hubert deferred flatteringly to her opinion, or rather asked her for a verdict. "I say, that's pretty stunning—isn't it?" he said in front of a Manet, and exclaimed when faced by one of the pictures of London painted by Monet: "Would you believe it, Westminster Bridge, I thought these chaps only painted French scenes." A Renoir of naked bathers prompted him to a slight abbreviated laugh. "Case where one averts the head and hurries on past. On the other hand I suppose it's art. What d'you think, any good?" When she said she liked it the thin head wavered on the stalk neck as he nodded. "It *is* art, that's what you've got to remember. I say Judy, I'm jolly glad I'm going round this show with you, I'd be lost otherwise."

Did she have a vague realization even then that most young

men didn't talk like this, that Hubert was, as Johnny Hatter might have put it, only fifty cards in the pack? Probably not, and even more than twenty years afterwards she could not be sure that was true. Hubert had at the time a job as a trainee in a merchant bank obtained by Uncle Puffin pulling strings. Later on he left the bank, joined a firm of numismatists (he had always been as interested in coins as his father was in carved wooden boxes) and become a partner in it—the partnership bought, Judith heard, by his father. He had married, now lived in Redhill, and was the senior partner in the firm, something she had learned from a coin collector in Wyfleet. The man was impressed that she knew Hubert, said he was a big wheel in the trade, had a high reputation. So perhaps he was a full pack after all, which made it worse.

They took a taxi back to Islington, and on the way back Hubert suddenly drew her to him, kissed her and tried to put his tongue in her mouth. She had never been kissed in that way before and was both startled and frightened. He stopped at once, was apologetic. "Don't know what got into me, must have been those pictures. Most awfully sorry, such a jolly little outing, now I've spoiled it." He was again the funny awkward Hubert she liked so much. It seemed somehow an additional apology that he tripped over the doorstep when they returned, went sprawling, ended up on the hall floor, and beamed up at her as if for approval.

After that there were other outings. They went to Kew Gardens, to the cinema, to a pop concert which she liked but at which Hubert was fidgety, saying that it gave him a funny feeling in his tummy. He treated her as if she were a younger sister; there was no more kissing. Uncle Puffin said it did her good to get out and about a bit and perhaps—here he glanced at Aunt Lilian—it did Hubert good too. Her nose twitched a little at the end as she asked what he meant.

"Why simply, my dear, simply and only, it's just that, I mean, Hubert doesn't, ah, seem to see many girls."

"I don't know why you should say that."

"Why, ah, he's never brought anybody home. So taking Judith about a little might, you could say, get him into the habit."

"Hubert is very young." The nose directed itself at Judith. "It's kind of him to take you to these exhibitions and concerts. I hope you appreciate it." She said she did.

When she looked back on this twenty years later, she wondered at it all. Uncle Puffin and Aunt Lilian seemed to her later view like people from another age, their standards and way of behaviour Edwardian or even Victorian, removed from modern life. How could she have endured the way Lilian spoke of her as if she were a being of a lower order? But she had remained for years dazed by the loss of her parents and her home (she never considered the Islington house as home), and she was not a natural rebel. She was not persecuted but life was dull, and years of dullness seemed to stretch ahead of her, with Hubert's presence the only alleviation. Lilian was a keen bridge player and belonged to a club where she spent two or three evenings a week. Uncle Puffin's life at the Ministry was for the most part easy so that he was home by five o'clock, but there were occasions when he worked late and ate dinner at his club, the Reform. It was on an evening when bridge playing and dinner at the Reform coincided that what she later thought of as inevitable happened. A casserole had been left in the oven, and when she took it out she burned her hand so that she cried out, and Hubert came running into the kitchen. He was upset to see her crying with pain, flapped his hands and looked about to burst into tears himself. She told him the ointment to get from the medicine cupboard, he rushed away, returned with a childish look of triumph, and put the ointment on what was after all only a slight burn. Then he put an arm round her, kissed her, and this time she did not protest when his tongue entered her mouth. When he suggested they should have a bit of a romp upstairs she put the casserole back into the oven, turned the gas very low, and went with him to his bedroom which was opposite hers on the top floor.

When he said with a giggle as they bounced about on the bed that if she felt inside his trousers she would find his third leg she did so, and was not shocked or surprised because girls at school had told her about erections, and when he said they should play mummies and daddies that did not shock her either. She did not know what to expect, and so again was not surprised that there was a lot of fumbling about, but a couple of older girls who had done it had said it hurt so she was pleased to find this was not so, and that it was in fact extremely pleasant. Afterwards Hubert, beaming a little fatuously, said, "That was a jolly old romp, wasn't it?" and then with a giggle, "I say, it's the first time I've done it properly." They went down to the kitchen and ate casserole, and then did it again.

Hubert did not need to tell her that Uncle Puffin and Aunt Lilian should be kept in the dark about what became a regular activity that took place not only when Lilian was playing bridge and Puffin working late but also, daringly, at night when she would cross the landing and they did it, speaking in murmurs, stifling giggles and cries. She did not tell girls at school, not even those supposed to have done it, in part because she felt they would not believe her, in part because the fact that nobody knew was part of the pleasure. Another part of it was that although Hubert was ten years her elder, she felt almost as she were his mother. He was so gentle, anxious, eager to prove his adequacy, that she found her role a protective one. He needed constant reassurance that this time had been as good as the last. She found she enjoyed the pretence that she was a real mummy and Hubert was her naughty son, and he played up to her, becoming quite reckless sometimes in giggling and talking so that she had to put a hand over his mouth to stop him. It was a fit of giggling that brought disaster. When she put a hand over Hubert's face to stop him, he bit it. She yelped quite loudly, then put a hand over her own mouth. They were both convulsed with laughter when Lilian opened the door, switched on the light.

They blinked at her like rabbits at car headlights.

She stared at them, raised her arm as if to cover her eyes, turned, disappeared. By the time she had been replaced by Puffin, Judith was back in her own room, sitting on the edge of the bed. He shook his head sorrowfully.

"Bad business," he said. "Won't do, won't do at all."

Just how bad a business it was became clear to her on the following morning. Uncle Puffin did not go to the Ministry, Hubert to his merchant bank, she to school. They were physical presences in the long dark drawing room, but it was Lilian who acted as prosecuting counsel, defence counsel and judge. Defence counsel spoke only on behalf of Hubert, to the effect that he had been deceived by a girl taken in out of charity, a girl who had betrayed the trust placed in her. The sentence was that she could no longer stay in the house. She would be found a lodging of some kind, but this branch of the family could no longer be responsible for the expense of her upbringing, and no other branch would be likely to take on such a burden. She was fourteen, quite old enough in prosecuting counsel's view to go out to work, and must now fend for herself.

At this point, Puffin intervened. Their chairs were grouped in a semi-circle round Lilian, and all three of them had listened to her relentless voice as it told the story of ingratitude and treachery. Uncle Puffin stared down at his elegant black boots, Hubert wriggled on his chair and sometimes looked as if about to cry. He did not speak, and Judith also said nothing. She felt a burning sensation within her that seemed in need of some verbal outlet, as she had felt the need to speak or cry out when making love. Yet if Hubert did not speak, what was there for her to say?

Now Puffin looked up from his boots. "Can't do that, wouldn't be the thing. Anyway, the law says Judy's got to be at school till she's sixteen."

His wife reared back like a snake unexpectedly attacked. "And was what she did the *thing?*"

Puffin's head wobbled on its stalk. "Can't say Judy did it, not much more than a child, Hubert's surely partly responsible. Can't be done anyway, wouldn't look good. Colleagues might hear of it, wouldn't like that."

"So what do *you* suggest?"

"Quite agree Hubert and Judy had better be—ah—be parted, not in the same house. Might be a good idea for Hubert to be on his own."

"And the girl stay here, is that your idea? I cannot believe my ears." Lilian's small, neat ears, usually as pale as the rest of her face barring the nose, had turned bright red.

"Not at all, wouldn't do, quite see that. Probably arrange for her to stay with a colleague, make some excuse, sure it's possible to come to an arrangement. Much the best way."

At this the burning sensation within Judy became so intense that she did speak, not to the elders arranging her future but to Hubert. "How can you let them decide? Why don't you say something?"

He did not look at her as he mumbled, "Very sorry for causing so much trouble."

Now she did not speak but cried out. "I'll tell you some more trouble, then. I'm pregnant."

She did not know what effect she had expected from the announcement except to make them take notice of her and include her in the discussion. This did not happen, however. Puffin said, "Oh, good Lord," Hubert burst into tears and said to nobody in particular that he was terribly sorry, Lilian told her husband almost triumphantly, "She plotted it, just look at her face." They then began to argue about whether she had plotted it, and if the family doctor would agree to sign the consent form for an abortion without asking awkward questions about the father. She found this unbearable, ran from the room, packed a case, left the house, and took a train to the only people she could think of, the Noons.

When she thought back on it, she wondered at the kindness of Emily Noon and her husband. She arrived distraught and barely coherent, but they accepted her without asking immediate questions, put her to bed, told Islington (she thought of her uncle, aunt and Hubert now simply as Islington, no longer as individuals) that she would be staying with them for a long visit. They were a conventional couple, but if they were shocked by her pregnancy they did not say so. Emily talked to her with an earnest stolidity about arranging an abortion if she wanted it, but although she had nothing but contempt for Hubert she yearned to see the creature growing inside her. The need for a decision vanished when she had the first of her miscarriages, one that she had of course never mentioned to Victor. Afterwards Emily kissed her, said it was for the best. "You've had a bad time. Now you must forget it all and enjoy yourself." But she had never forgotten and, as she felt now, never enjoyed herself. At sixteen she left the state school in Wyfleet and took a course in shorthand and typing. She got a job in a solicitor's office as an audio typist but hated the legal rigmarole, and then saw Lassiter's advertisement in the local paper for a junior typist.

Most of this she told Billy Gay in what she absurdly thought of as their room at the Marvin, the dingy room she felt she knew so well, with its dark oak dressing table and the mirror above it that had a slight crack at the top and a rash of what looked like rust spots halfway down, the repp curtains that did not pull across properly, the little bathroom smelling of antiseptic. He heard her almost without interruption, hand behind his head, looking up at the ceiling, occasionally giving her his sideways glance. When she told him about the advertisement he said, "You married the boss's son."

"If that's the way it sounds, yes, I suppose so." He put a hand on hers, said sorry. "No need to be, only it didn't seem like that. I always got on well with Victor, he was nice to me from the start. I was frightened of his father, the Old Man as Victor called him, and he liked that. My being frightened of the Old Man, I mean, because he was too. The Old Man wasn't pleased when we got married. I'd been there two years then."

"Rough time. Sound like real bastards, your aunt and uncle. Ever hear from them?"

"They're both dead now, it was twenty years ago. I think Uncle Puffin paid some money to the Noons when I was at school. All a long time ago. Just about when you were born." He smiled at her, lighted a cigarette. "They never wrote to me, didn't come to the wedding though Victor insisted they should be asked, didn't send a present. Hubert sent one, a set of fish knives and forks, silver plated. Funny really." He smiled again, dutifully perhaps. "And he wrote to me after I ran away, Hubert I mean. Said he was sorry I felt I had to leave, but perhaps it was for the best. Sent a check for fifty pounds, thought I might need it. I always thought my uncle put him up to it. I sent the check back torn up."

"That right? Tearing up money, you got to have it to do that."

She shook her head vigorously. "I wasn't rich, I was poor. Don't you see it was an insult, the worst they could offer me. As if they were buying me off, and thought they could do it for fifty pounds."

"Yeah, well, okay if you say so, but I don't see it. You got to have money to think like that. You been abroad?"

"Yes, Victor and I have often been for summer holidays in Italy, France, Spain."

"America?" She said no. "Reckon I'd like it there, California 'specially. I seen the ads, it looks fantastic. No restrictions like here, class and that, take you for what you are, you got money to spend, you're in. More millionaires than anywhere else in America they say."

"You'd find it isn't like that. If you don't get the plum jobs, or any job at all, you just go under."

"Fair enough. I'd like to give it a try."

"Billy, what do you think about me?" She knew the question

was foolish, but could not refrain from asking it. "Going to bed with you, I mean."

"Told you, di'nt I? You're fantastic."

"Yes, but you must have wondered, why am I doing it? I mean, what's wrong with my marriage? I ask myself, because you see in a way there's nothing wrong, Victor's attractive or most women think so. I don't know what it is, he's not like you, he doesn't—he's not like you."

He stubbed out his cigarette. "Not my business. Look, like I said, you're fantastic, leave it that way. Or is it you're saying move in with you, that what you mean?"

She said, astonished, "Of course not. Nothing like that."

"Okay then, leave it. It's good, innit, been good today?" She nodded. "So take it the way it is, makes you happy, I like it too. Leave it."

So she left it.

3

Something about the routine of shopping in a large super-market like the Wyfleet Safeway attracted her. There was a distinct emotional satisfaction to be found in moving from aisle to aisle, from washing powders through kitchen goods to cooked meats and cheeses, loading the trolley with things some of which were essential, others only possibly useful, wavering between half a dozen French cheeses, taking a packet of breadsticks and then discarding them for some toasted biscuits called Thinnies. Around her were other trolley pushers equally absorbed in their quests, hesitating in front of the salad dressings, taking the cartons of ready packed meals. She went to the supermarket in the early afternoon before the busy time, when shoppers were unhurried, man or woman and trolley seeming linked in a union broken only when they went through the automatic doors, unloaded what they had brought into cars, returned to life. The supermarket seemed to her a kind of fairyland, a make-believe world insu-lated from the problems and pleasures of life, remote equally from the ordered world of Green Diamonds and the rust-spotted mirror and dingy carpets of the Marvin. Even its air-conditioned coolness emphasized the unlikeness to the slightly sticky, faintly oppressive summer heat outside. She hesitated as she approached the magic doors, reluctant to go through the check-out and leave fairyland.

"Fancy a cup of char?"

For a moment she did not recognize him, then thought: of course, the policeman, Craxton. He sported only a wire basket with a few things in it, not a well-filled trolley. Reluctance to leave the supermarket made her say yes, and she followed him to what he called the caff at one end of the store, past wines, spirits and mineral waters, where a few shoppers sat on plastic chairs at formica-topped tables. He left his basket with her as he went up to the self-service counter to get what he described as tea and a wad. His basket contained a small packet of washing powder, paper napkins, a couple of tins. When he came back she said, "You live on your own."

He grinned. "Detective, eh? Could be my wife's away, or I'm shopping for a neighbour. You're right though. Divorced, been on my own for a few months. Not easy being married to a policeman, as my wife often told me. In the end she decided it was too difficult, moved in with a manager of a firm selling conservatories, office job, regular hours. Couldn't blame her really, parted on good terms. No kids, that didn't help." He bit into a dismal-looking bun. "Like you."

"How do you know that?"

"Told you before, I know things. It's my job."

"I don't see it can be any of your business whether or not I have children."

"You might be right," he said as if conceding a point. "Just something I happen to know. Told you before, I'm interested in you. Said you were the most attractive woman at that shin-dig the other week. I could extend it to this emporium."

As she said flattery would get him nowhere she was conscious of the flirtatiousness of her manner, and wondered at it. Billy says I'm fantastic, she thought, and now this police-man seems to be serious when he calls me attractive, perhaps it's true. She became aware she had missed something he was saying and said sorry, her thoughts had wondered.

"I said, it's personal but professional too. The interest."

"I don't know what that means."

"You understood the personal bit, that's for sure. I don't have to spell it out." As she looked at the tough worn face, the scar on his cheek that today had a faint colour, the dark eyes, she felt a force in him that made her uneasy yet was somehow pleasant, not at all the feeling she had when with Billy. Or with Victor, for that matter. "The other is something I wouldn't be telling you but for that. You know about Burley Common."

"The plan for new houses, yes. Victor's the architect. There's some trouble about it with the Council."

"Right. That all you know?"

She decided not to say anything about young Nethersole, and nodded her head.

"Good for you. But you can tell your husband this. Say you met me, say I'd had one or two and opened my mouth wider than I should if you like, or say I fancy you, which would be the truth but might not be what he wanted to hear. Anyway, drop the word I said there was trouble brewing, and he should keep his nose clean. You got that?"

"Trouble about Burley Common?"

"That's part of it. A bit of it."

"What are the other parts?"

He shook his head. "That's the message. Something I'm passing on which I shouldn't. Because of you. Keep his nose clean. If it's dirty get a handkerchief and wipe it."

She looked again at the few things in his basket. "You didn't have to come in here to get those, you could have got them anywhere. You followed me in."

"Don't let your imagination run away with you. The paper napkins here are something special."

"You followed me in. Just to tell me this."

He grinned at her again. "Don't forget what I said at the start. The interest is personal."

4

When she got back to Green Diamonds the telephone was ringing. The sound continued up to the moment she picked up the receiver, when it changed to the buzz of an empty line. As she brought in her supermarket purchases and put them away she worried about the call, convincing herself it was something that called for immediate action. Victor had been involved in an accident and was in hospital, or Debbie was calling to say her husband had seen Judith going into the Marvin with Billy, or Billy telling her that since she didn't want to move in with him he thought they should call it a day. Or—the telephone rang again.

Victor's voice said, "He's gone." For a moment she did not understand. "The Old Man. He's gone. One o'clock today, punctually at one, time for lunch now, he used to say. I've been trying to get you, where were you?" He seemed not to hear her reply, repeated that it had been one o'clock, said he couldn't believe it. She found herself irritated. What was it he found hard to believe? Surely the Old Man had been waiting to die, and they had been waiting on his death, for years now. She tried to say something like that without harshness, but he interrupted. "You don't understand, you simply don't understand what he meant to me." When she suggested he should come home he said, in a voice unlike the one she knew, a voice full of despair, that there were things to do in the office, arrangements to make for the funeral.

If she had thought the failure of breath in that frail body was the last she would hear of the Old Man, she soon realized her mistake. The *Express and News*, the local rival to the *Mercury*, had a column on the front headed "Famous Architect Dies" and a whole page of tributes and photographs inside. At the funeral, fifty cars followed the hearse to St. Luke's Church, which was packed with people to hear the vicar saying George St. John Lassiter had been not only an architect concerned with the grace and style and fitness of the buildings he designed, but also a man who by the unshakeable dignity of his bearing and the unswerving integrity of his life had been raised above our common humanity, even though he was in all things finely human. Victor, beside her, shifted uneasily, his shoulders shaking with emotion. Judith wondered if the vicar had known the Old Man, whether any of it was perhaps true. Her thoughts strayed, she had a vision of herself on the bed in the Marvin, crying out with pleasure. She closed her eyes tightly dismissing the vision. Victor placed a hand over hers consolingly.

The baked meats were eaten not at Green Diamonds but in a recently built extension to the Golf Club. Debbie, wearing a black dress made of some shiny material and a rather fetching black hat with a red feather in it, took her arm and said she shouldn't look so miserable, it would soon be over. When Judith said she hadn't known she was looking miserable, Debbie considered her more carefully.

"Maybe I'm wrong, not miserable, more as if you're not here. You never liked him, did you? I don't know I'd have wanted him for a father-in-law, but he was a wonderful old bugger." She looked at Judith's dark grey dress. "You didn't exactly dress up, did you?"

"Why should I? I'm not sorry he's dead."

"Mustn't say things like that about the dear departed. You should circulate, darling, it's your party."

She spoke to Clive Braden, who said George had been a wonderful architect and a fine man, and nodded to Eleanor whose nose was raised permanently in the air as she murmured something about Victor's father bein' very charmin' when she sat next to him one evenin' at a dinner given by the RIBA at the Royal Academy. Then it was Johnny, in a dark suit and black tie, who asked how Victor was taking it. "I know he was devoted to the Old Man. I was too, respected him anyway. Hard man to deal with though, hard on you too I daresay. Thought you weren't right for his only son."

" 'Not good enough' might be the phrase."

"You said it, not me. Victor's cut up, no doubt about it. Needs looking after. Had to happen, though, and this is a pretty good time." It was in her mind to ask what he meant by looking after Victor, but instead she said she didn't understand why he should think this was a good time. "I suppose Victor will inherit, and the Old Man must have been pretty comfortable."

"I suppose so."

"Might solve a few problems then."

The obsequies seemed to her endless, although in fact it was no more than a couple of hours before the last hand was shaken, the last words of praise said. Back again in Green Diamonds she asked Victor what Johnny Hatter had meant.

"It's no secret there's a cash flow problem at the moment, everyone's got it. You remember I told the Old Man the last time we saw him. Whisky?" His hand was on the decanter. She shook her head, asked if that was all. He said of course it was.

"Nethersole and his son, what's happened about that?"

"Nothing yet. It isn't important, sorry I told you. I can't talk about things like that now, you should understand." His smile switched on then off, like a lighthouse beam. "Stupid, I know, but I've been knocked sideways."

She suddenly remembered Craxton's message, which had been put out of her head by the Old Man's death and the funeral. She told him what the policeman had said, and Victor's look changed from laughing charmer to petulant little boy, the look she had seen when he was being rebuked by the Old Man. She asked what Craxton had meant.

"How should I know? I don't understand why you were talking to him. All right, I know you were at the same school when you were five years old but you needn't make him your bosom friend now, surely."

"I was ten years old, not five, when I left Cross Lanes, and of course he's not a bosom friend. I told you I met him in the supermarket, and I think he followed me to give that message, though I can't be sure."

"You really think so? And your judgement's better than mine." He put down his glass, came over, and kissed her cheek. The smile reappeared and this time stayed on, no lighthouse beam. "What it means is Craxton's an interfering so-and-so who's sticking his nose in where he shouldn't. I might get Clive to have a word with the Chief Constable."

"Could it be something to do with Nethersole?"

"Of course not. I told you Nethersole's not important. I really don't know what he meant, but it's nothing to worry about. I've been a miserable sod lately, I'm sorry, it's been a bad week or two. Shall we see what's on the box?"

They saw what was on the box. In bed that night she thought about the conversation and realized he had given no explanation of what the words might mean. But speculation faded in the aching need she felt for Billy Gay. She had rung Ron Hinks after Victor told her of the Old Man's death, spoken to Billy and told him she would not be able to see him for a few days, but would get in touch as soon as she was free. His side

of the conversation had been confined to "Yeah" and "Okay."
When, at the end, she had said both as a warning and a joke,
"Don't ring me, I'll ring you," he had responded with another
"Okay," and it occurred to her that he might have been upset.
She longed to see him, and explain, but until Victor returned
to the office, did not dare to ring again. In the meantime she
summoned up every feature of him, neat smallish head, well-
shaped mouth, pale unblemished torso, flat stomach, slim
tapering thighs and between them the penis from which even
now she was inclined to avert her eyes. She told herself that
the longing she felt was not sexual, although she knew this to
be untrue.

On the following day Victor went back to the office. At
breakfast he was his usual smiling self, unlike the shaky hol-
low-eyed figure she had seen across the table since the Old
Man's death. The smile, the eagerness with which he ate his
croissants, and the blue and white spotted bow tie that replaced the plain black one he had worn for a week, all seemed
signals that he was determined to put away the past. She was
touched, but still she telephoned Ron Hinks, to be told that
Billy was engaged with a client. She had taken the ridiculous
precaution of speaking through a piece of cloth to disguise her
voice, but she did not want to leave her number, and said she
would call again.

On this morning she found the photographs.

She was looking for a handkerchief, a Swiss linen handkerchief she particularly liked, which had a hand-embroidered
border. She remembered ironing it, but could not find it
where it should have been, in her bedroom chest of drawers.
It occurred to her that the handkerchief might have been left
on the ironing board, and been put away by Patty with Victor's
shirts and other things. (She later found the handkerchief
tucked away by Patty inside a pair of her own pants.) But the
drawer in Victor's pine chest held only what it should have
done, his handkerchiefs placed neatly to one side, socks on
the other. She pulled the handle of the drawer next to it

without thinking, because she knew this drawer was kept locked. Victor had said once that he felt a desk to be an inappropriate obtrusion in a private house, and she understood that he kept in this drawer things that he vaguely said shouldn't be left lying about.

So she was surprised when, at her involuntary gesture, this drawer opened, and she saw lying at the very top of it a revolver. After a moment she recognized it as the Mauser the Old Man had, by his account, related to Victor and passed on by Victor to her, taken off a German during the War. Shortly after their marriage Victor had joined a shooting club, and the Old Man had given him the Mauser as some kind of encouragement, or a mark of approval. Victor had, however, resigned from the club after a few visits convinced him that he was a very poor shot. Below the revolver were a lot of papers, but no handkerchief. She could not resist, never thought of resisting, looking at the papers.

On the top was a bunch of letters with a rubber band round them. She recognized the Old Man's neat hand, skimmed through a couple of them, saw they had been written in Victor's schooldays and contained censorious remarks about his laziness, blended with praise of his intelligence and quickness. "There is no substitute for an integrity of mind in which I find you lacking. Your report remarks as I have done on your cleverness, but also your lack of application." Why had Victor kept all this stuff? Another rubber band held a smaller packet of four letters from someone who signed himself "Jerry." These were undated, but evidently more recent than those from the Old Man. She recalled Victor mentioning a university friend named Jerry Comber who had joined some sort of monastic order, and that this was the same Jerry was confirmed by a snap showing a bulky figure wearing a long robe, and on his head what looked like a chimney cowl. These letters were sent from the Congo, where Jerry was evidently a member of something like a Christian Aid mission, and they were concerned with the difficulty of obtaining medical supplies. A phrase or two caught her attention. ". . . pointless to regret the past, and I do remember you with great affection, but what I'm doing here affords complete fulfillment. Can you say the same, or anything like it?" Another letter suggested Victor should come out and see what was being done, a third congratulated him on his marriage, and said, "I hope it may be a solution for you, as the work here has been for me." On the back of the snap Victor had written in a dashing calligraphy quite unlike his father's: "Jerry died of enteric fever October '78. A saint."

She put the band back round these letters, wondered whether they had a homosexual relationship, and found she was not surprised or shocked. After all, she thought, they say everybody has sexual feelings towards their own sex at some time, and it was all long ago. She couldn't recall experiencing such feelings herself, and so far as she knew none of her Wyfleet friends was homosexual or lesbian, but perhaps she was innocent about the behaviour of people she knew. She contemplated this last proposition, and decided that if any activities of that kind went on Debbie would know about them, and would have told her. Beneath the letters were bank statements she didn't bother to look at, insurance policies for the house and for their cars, their two wills made five years ago, in which each left all they possessed to the other. She remembered Victor laughing and saying she hadn't anything to leave, which she supposed was true.

At the bottom of the drawer was a manilla envelope and a small cardboard box. She opened the box first and found it contained a dozen bullets, presumably for the Mauser. Then she opened the envelope.

In it were six photographs. They were larger than postcard size, eight inches by five perhaps, and when she looked at them she found she could after all be both surprised and shocked. They were good prints, with a freshness that showed they had been taken recently, in the last year or two.

The first photograph showed Victor and another man, both

naked. Victor was kneeling, and had the man's penis in his mouth. The man was young, perhaps in his early twenties, a brutishly powerful rather than handsome figure. One hand was placed firmly on Victor's head. The same man appeared in three of the other photographs, in the remaining two an older man with tattoos on his chest and arms. In all of them Victor's role was submissive. In one his hands were tied behind his back, and the tattooed man stood above him holding a cane.

She looked at the photographs for what seemed a long time, changing one for another as if they were playing cards. Then she put five of them back in the envelope, keeping out the one she had first looked at, and returned everything to the drawer exactly as it had been. She rang Ron Hinks's garage again, this time making no attempt to conceal her voice, spoke to Billy and said she wanted to see him.

"You'd like an appointment," he said, so that she knew somebody else must be there. "Yeah, okay. When you want to make it?"

"This afternoon."

"Sorry, afternoon's fully booked."

"This evening then."

A pause, then the voice that conveyed so little of his youth and gentleness said, "Sorry, can't do that, 'fraid."

She said pleadingly: "Billy."

Another pause. "Sorry, but it's no can do. You wanna book another refresher course we could start tomorrow, three o'clock."

Almost in a whisper she said, "All right, three o'clock tomorrow. At our hotel."

When she put down the receiver she was shaking. I wanted to see him today, she thought, wanted that more than anything else in the world. He can't have cared about seeing me or he'd have put off whatever he was doing. Then she thought that was unjust and wondered what she would say to him. She thought of telephoning Debbie, decided against it, but found it intolerable to stay in the house. She got out the Fiesta, drove into town, and went to the charity shop. It was not one of her days for working there but the ladies were delighted to see her. She spent much of the afternoon listening to Mrs. Butterworth's stories about her three-year-old grandson, who had stuck a button up his nose and when that was removed had bitten a glass, swallowed some of the smaller fragments and been rushed off to hospital, from which he had emerged apparently none the worse. When she got back to Green Diamonds the Lagonda was in the drive, Victor on the deck looking at an architectural magazine. It was the laughing charmer who greeted her, said he was sorry he'd got a little hot under the collar when she told him about speaking to Craxton, asked if she felt like going out to eat tonight. She said something, she did not know what, as she walked past him down the corridor to her bedroom, and returned with the photograph. She showed it to him, said, "I found this."

Victor looked at it, then at her. He entered the living room, and when she followed him, carefully closed the plate glass door, then asked where she had found the photograph.

"In your chest of drawers, the drawer wasn't locked, I was looking for one of my handkerchiefs." She was conscious of gabbling, perhaps sounding ridiculous.

"May I have it please." He held out a hand. She was aware that her voice rose, as she asked if he had nothing else to say. He touched his little moustache. "You snooped and found something you shouldn't have. What do you expect me to say?" He put the photograph face down on a small table.

"I expect—" She did not know what she expected. "It disgusts me, this and the others, they disgust me." She went on, "I want to know who this man is. And the other man. I suppose there have been others too. I want to know about them, I want you to explain."

"I'd sooner not talk about it, but if we're going to, let's sit down." He did so, apparently at ease, one leg cocked over the other, a great deal of sock and an inch of leg showing.

101

"The people, well, they're just people who share my tastes, one of them lives in London, the other's in the navy. The one who lives in London is an amateur photographer."

"Having photographs taken, you must be out of your mind. They could blackmail you."

"A bit rash perhaps, but there are times when one just longs for the record of a particular moment. I daresay you won't understand that, but it's true. Blackmail, though, no I don't think so. Billy would be very vulnerable himself, and the others, like the one with the tattoos, don't know me from Adam." The charmer smile. "Though they would know me from Eve."

"Billy, did you say his name was Billy?" She shuddered.

"That's right. Why? I can assure you you don't know him."

"Nothing." She sat looking down at the carpet. "I suppose this, this sort of thing, has gone on for a long time." He did not reply. "Our marriage, it's been a sham. A marriage of convenience."

"That isn't true at all. Look at me." She raised her head. His face was set in a serious expression. "I love you, I mean it when I say that. If we'd had children things might have been different."

"You're saying it's my fault?"

"Of course not, just that children might have affected things, I don't know. What I'm saying is I value you, rely on you, you're important to me, I thought you realized it."

"But you don't love me. Unless you can force me to make love. Or force yourself."

"I do love you." His tone was the patient one of a doctor explaining something to a slightly obtuse patient. "I love you, I love being married to you, I don't love anybody else. I remember to send roses. We're a partnership, been through all sorts of things together. But there are limits to every partnership, things it's best not to know about anybody." He touched his bow tie. "You could say these are drawers it's better to keep locked, perhaps you have a locked drawer yourself. Anyway, I'm very sorry I left mine open. It was stupid, careless, I apologize. I'm asking you to forget it."

"Forget it," she said unbelievingly. "And you'd just go on doing those things. No, I'm sorry but I can't do that. Perhaps I'm out of date, old-fashioned, but I can't do it, not now I know. You say there are things you can't control, and there are for me too." She repeated with passionate emphasis, "It disgusts me, you understand. What you do disgusts me."

He nodded, and said with the calmness that had at first surprised and was now angering her. "So what do you suggest?"

If she could have put things clearly she would have said: I don't suggest, I know. What I know is that I don't want this house and this life, I have never wanted them, I want to go back to Doyle Street and a house with numbers, I wanted a simple life as a mother with children and, although there can never be children, I still want that simple life, but more than all those things I want to be loved and to love in return, and you have never given me that kind of love or I given it to you, but now I think I have found it and I can't let it go. However, she said nothing like that. The words that came from her mouth, words that surprised her even as she uttered them, were: "I want a divorce."

When he repeated "divorce" with the apparently calculating calmness that angered her, she said it more confidently. "You must give me a divorce. Then you can do what you like, have your sailor and the others here to stay if that's what you want." She did not care to mention the name Billy.

"I shouldn't like that." At that she cried out and asked if he thought she liked what she had learned. He repeated patiently, "I shouldn't like it, I'll tell you why. Some of the people I deal with are perfectly all right, don't mind what you do as long as you don't frighten the horses. But the others, some of them, Rotary Club people, they wouldn't like it.

When there's a divorce rumours get around, and Wyfleet isn't London. It would be bad for business. Among other problems."

She couldn't believe what she heard. "So I'm to stay married to you because if we were divorced it would be bad for business. That's a pity, but you'll just have to put up with it."

"I don't think so. I wouldn't let you do it. I should contest it."

She felt a well of anger inside herself at his confidence, his calmness. "And have evidence in court about what you do with your friends, or whatever you call them. Wouldn't that be bad for business?" He shook his head. "Don't fool yourself that I wouldn't—" she began, but was checked by his next words.

"I said we all have locked drawers. I know what's in yours." Was it possible he knew about Billy Gay? She was soon undeceived. "You wouldn't like the details of what you got up to with Hubert Delaware brought out in court, would you? About how a little tart—that was what your aunt called you— seduced him, and deliberately got herself pregnant to try to force him to marry her. I don't think you'd like all that dirty linen washed in public. Your uncle and aunt told me about it when I went to ask their blessing on our marriage. Do you know what the Old Man said when I told him? She's got no money and she's a strumpet. Then he said perhaps a strumpet might be good for me, what I needed. It didn't work out like that, though, did it?" Sounding suddenly like the Old Man he said, "No use turning on the waterworks, I'm telling you the facts. You black my eye, I'll black yours."

What she fastened on was the central, incredible thing. "You knew. You always knew. When you were being sympathetic, and I thought you liked me, loved me, you just felt sorry for me. Was that it?"

He said almost indifferently: "If you like."

"But it wasn't the way you're saying. Hubert was so kind and nice, my aunt was awful, I hardly knew what I was doing.

You must believe that. I mean, you must have believed it then."

He said soothingly, "Of course I did. Otherwise I wouldn't have wanted to marry you. I still believe it. I'm just telling you the way it would come out. You can imagine the sort of questions you'd be asked."

"And you'd do that, make me suffer like that?" He looked at her steadily, did not answer. "You not only disgust me, I despise you."

His fingers touched his bow tie, for the first time he showed signs of impatience. "You're being hysterical about this, hysterical and stupid. Try to be reasonable."

"*Reasonable*? After the way you threatened me you talk about being reasonable?"

"You threatened me, I reacted. But I don't want to react, please believe that. I meant it when I said we were a partnership, one like Harold Nicholson and Vita Sackville-West if you like. There are things that go on outside a partnership, and I'm asking you to accept them. And to believe our marriage is important to me."

"Yes, it helps with the Rotary Club."

"I shouldn't have said that, but yes, it has a business importance. And I shan't let you break it."

"Just try and stop me." She got up, walked down the corridor and into her room, locking herself in. A minute or two later she heard his footsteps. The door handle turned.

"We'll talk about it in the morning." She did not answer. "When you've had time to think."

In the night she did have time to think. She saw herself in the witness box, saw the tall whey-faced sneering man she envisaged as Victor's counsel, a man like some actor on television, asking questions about Hubert, about what other sexual experiences she had had before him, whether she had enjoyed them, if she felt her attitude towards sexual relations in her own marriage had always been—how should he put it?—fully cooperative? And then, the climactic moment, the whey-faced

105

man's sneer would change to a smirk as he asked: "Do you know a hotel named the Marvin, Mrs. Lassiter? Have you ever stayed there? Signing the register yourself in the not unusual name of Smith? And accompanied by the very youthful Mr. Smith?"

The scene was vivid and unbearable.

She remembered then what she had read about the hit man. Foster's plan had failed because the man he approached had given him away to the police. But she would be careful, she would make sure her hit man would never give her away. In a case of murder, the wife or husband is the first person to be suspected. So this must not be a case of murder . . .

In the morning, Victor asked if she had slept on it. She said she had. And? And she had decided to do nothing about it on condition Victor stopped seeing his friends, the ones in the photographs.

There were dark patches under Victor's blue eyes, but now those eyes sparkled, he came round the breakfast table and kissed the top of her head.

"You're a darling sensible girl. I told you last night, we're a partnership."

"And you'll stop seeing people like those prostitutes?"

"Harsh words. Not right, either. But since it's what you want, yes. I'm glad. We've been together too long to break up."

Did he believe what he was saying? It was of no importance anyway. She simply said yes.

5

She got to the Marvin a few minutes early. The toupeed ancient had been replaced by a square-jawed man with a heavy blue chin and a head so closely and crudely shaved that small scabs showed on it. When she signed the register he said, "Supposed to put an address." She said she had not done so before. Small cold eyes considered her, then he nodded. "Okay, they filled it in for you, I'll do it."

She was about to ask how they knew her address, then understood what he meant. "Can we have the room we had before, room six?"

"Why not, key's here." He gave it to her, face still stoney. In the room she looked once more at the damp stain, the peeling fruit-patterned wallpaper, noticed the cigarette stubs left in an ashtray and the soiled hand-towel in the bathroom and thought: this must end, I can't bear it. She knew also that she could not give up Billy Gay. The solution, then, was for Victor not to exist, and the key to that solution was the hit man. She thought about it as she sat on the bed, then examined herself in the cracked mirror, searching for the lines of age, biting her pale lips to give them colour. I look like a middle-aged housewife, she thought, and that's what I am. But when I take off my clothes I look younger, and not many middle-aged housewives can say that.

She looked at her watch, and saw it was ten past-three. A few minutes later she felt sure there had been a misunderstanding, he had gone to Green Diamonds, got tired of ringing the bell, returned to the garage. She went over the details of that telephone conversation, the way he had said, "Sorry, can't do that," and decided he was tired of her, had given her up. The tap on the door came at a quarter to four. When she opened it and saw him there she did not wait for an explanation, but burst into tears and clung to him. The reproaches in her mind stayed unuttered, instead she said in broken phrases that she loved him, longed to see him, terrible things had been happening.

"Hold on," he said. "Thought you sounded het up on the blower. So what's up?"

She blew her nose, wiped her eyes. "God, I must look terrible. Why are you so late? I thought you weren't coming."

"Couldn't be helped. Out with some stupid cow, not this refresher lark just a driving lesson, came up to a light she puts her clodhopping great feet on the accelerator 'stead of the brake, runs up into a Cavalier in front. He wasn't pleased, she had hysterics, Ron says shoulda stopped her with the dual. All right, I tells him, you try using the bleeding dual when some old cow's got her foot down trying to get up to ninety's though she's in a bleeding film. He moans on and on about what it's costing him and I said whatsamatter you're insured, and he says yeah but he'll be missing a car while this one's being done up. So then I says a few more things, the way it ends Ron says don't bother to come back. You had a bad night, I've had a bleeding terrible day." He sat on the bed, face in hands, looking about fifteen. Then he said, "Sorry about the language," and she shivered with delight. She asked if he would go down to the Job Center.

"Not likely. See what I can pick up, mates of mine want a spare driver sometimes, do this and that. I don't want to fill no forms so they get your number. Pity though, it was money for old rope." He patted the bed. "Come here." She sat beside him and he kissed her, not angrily or passionately but gently, then said, "Now you tell me, what's up?"

When it came to the point she found it difficult, not difficult to say what Victor had been doing but to make him understand her revulsion.

"Okay, he's gay. No big deal."

"You said yourself how upset you were when you were a boy—"

"Yeah, right, I was just a kid, didn't want to be picked on. But now, I know a few gays, not real mates but I never had trouble with them."

"It isn't just that." She found it hard to say what it was. "He's—his whole life's a lie, he's been lying to me all the time we've been married."

He stroked her hand. "Don't get me wrong, but you're getting a bit of your own back, seems to me."

"Yes, but—" Why was it not the same? "The photographs, they were awful. He's a masochist I suppose, wants to be a slave and be forced to do things."

"Yeah, well, sooner him than me." He kissed her, pushed her down on the bed. "I don't want to be a slave, master neither. Just doing what comes naturally, letting yourself go, way I see it, suit you?"

She let herself go, and it suited her. Afterwards she felt serene, satisfied, as if her discovery about Victor was unimportant. Still, she knew that wasn't so. Love, as had occurred to her when driving to the Marvin that day, does not solve problems but creates them. And love makes demands too, demands that must be fulfilled if it is to survive. Her thoughts in the night had been so clear, the solution so obvious and necessary. Yet she knew that if she was to persuade Billy of that necessity she mustn't alarm him or upset him. He had to see the solution himself.

So she said carefully, "I told Victor I wanted a divorce, but he won't give me one."

He was smoking, blew a smoke ring. "That so, why not?"

"He says it would affect business, some of his Rotary clients wouldn't like it. I think really he's worried rumours might get around about the things he gets up to."

"Could be."

"He said he'd contest the case. It turns out he knows about what I told you the other day, about Hubert."

He seemed for a moment not to understand, then said, "Hubert, yeah, the abortion and that. And that old aunt of yours, never heard 'bout anyone like her. So he'd play rough, right."

"He might put an enquiry agent on to it who'd find out about us. You'd be brought into it, have to give evidence."

"That right? Okay, we agree what to say and I'd say it. What you wanted."

How could he be so foolish, fail so signally to understand what she was trying to convey without using crude, simple words? "I can't go on living with him."

"But he says no."

"*I can't go on*, do you understand?"

He threw back the bedclothes. "Got to do a pee."

When he came back he pulled on pants then stood confronting her, frowning a little. How could she have thought he looked ordinary at that first meeting, when now the sight of his body made her feel faint? He said, "Must be stupid, don't know what you're at, tell me."

She spoke carefully. "You and I, if we could be together all the time, would you like it?"

"Yeah, be great."

"If Victor wasn't there, we could be."

"Yeah?" he said on a questioning note. "Yeah, be good. Not on, though."

Why didn't he understand when it was so simple, so obvious, to her? She forced herself to go on. "You told me about your friends—you know, about your father. I thought you might know somebody . . ." Her voice faded, she was relieved when he nodded.

"I get you, only, see, that was special, Dad. I mean, like there was a reason, here they wouldn't have no reason, get me?" He corrected himself. "Wouldn't have a reason. If they did he'd still be there after, right? Put him in hospital, he'd come out again."

She tried to speak, couldn't manage it, gasped like a fish in air, then suddenly found words. "There'd be a reason. Whoever did it would be paid." The next words were harder, but she managed them. "And then we'd be together. What I thought was, afterwards he wouldn't be there at all."

Silence. His eyes, which looked directly at her, seemed to have become enormous. What was it she saw in them, alarm, astonishment, acceptance? She was not left long in doubt. "Hey, that's crazy stuff," he said.

At that, as if a spring had been released, words fairly tumbled from her, words saying he mustn't be personally involved, that wouldn't do at all, it must be somebody he knew of and not a friend, somebody who had done this kind of thing before or something like it, needed the money, and it must be planned carefully because of course it must have no connection with her either, an accident would be ideal, some kind of accident so that nothing was even suspected. As she talked he went on looking at her steadily, at the same time pulling on his clothes, the jeans and a T-shirt that said in big letters Up Yours. She finished weakly, dismayed by his expression.

"His father's dead, you saw that I expect, he was quite well off, Victor will inherit. We could travel, go to California, that was the place you wanted to see, anywhere."

He said again, "Crazy, just crazy. No way I'd do that stuff."

111

"I told you, it wouldn't be you."

"Yeah, yeah, some mate of mine you said. First thing, I got no mates into stuff like that, next if I did the filth'd soon be out he was my mate, get on to us in five minutes."

"You weren't listening properly. I said we'd have to find a way so that nobody would be suspected."

"And how you going to do that? Forget it." He came close to her, held her by the shoulders, shook her, not angrily but affectionately, as if he were fifteen years her senior instead of the other way round. "We got something good going, enjoy it. I go for you, you're my Judy, don't let's push it, right?"

She said hopefully, "There'd be money in it," stopped as he shook his head. "You won't even talk about it."

"Nothing to talk about. I'm never going inside again, told you that. Reckon we oughta be going."

She thought afterwards of things she might have said. She could have asked why he was in such a hurry when he had no job any more, could have started to take off his clothes or told him the hit man would get a lot of money, but she did none of them. Instead she asked when they would meet again, and he said he was going to put himself about trying to find something steady, he'd give her a bell and make sure it was on a weekday so she'd be alone. Afterwards she could think of nothing except that she had lost him.

AFTERWARDS

That's it then, is it?" Sergeant Ewbank said. "Made up our minds at last, have we? Taken long enough, wasted a lot of my time, cocker, you know that?"

"I'm sorry," Godfrey Jackson said, or more nearly whispered. "Sorry to have given so much trouble. It was just that having been in trouble before, I really thought—"

"You really thought you were unobserved and could get away with it. You know what you are, my lad, you're a bit pathetic. Right then, let's get it down."

Pathetic was a reasonable enough word for Godfrey Jackson. He was a timid thirty-year-old who lived with his widowed mother. Godfrey was in every way but one a model member of society, but the exception had time and again landed him in trouble. He could not resist stealing money when the chance arose. The sight of a jacket hung up in an office or locker room prompted him to look quickly for a wallet and extract any notes he found in it, a handbag or purse left lying on a seat for five minutes had a magnetic attraction for him. Left alone in a friend's house he would tiptoe upstairs to a bedroom and look around for any notes or coins that might have been left in jackets, wallets or purses.

Godfrey's friends (and he retained some, for he was an amiable little man) learned not to leave cash lying around, but men and women in the several offices where he worked as wages clerk, invoice clerk and assistant accountant were less cautious. At first he simply lost jobs when the thefts were discovered, then came up in court and was twice put on probation, eventually got a prison sentence. He readily, even eagerly accepted psychiatric treatment for what his mother called Godfrey's little weakness, which one psychiatrist attributed to the fact that he had been given no pocket money in childhood. Since he came out of prison eighteen months back Godfrey seemed to have been on the straight and narrow at the engineering works where the probation officer found him a job. When, however, one of the callers on the special line said he had seen a man running down Lover's Lane around eleven thirty on the morning of the murder and gave a description that more or less fitted Godfrey, he was called for questioning. He foolishly said he had been at work, but an enquiry at the engineering plant revealed that he had lost his job a week earlier when found in a locker room where office staff had no business to be, since it was reserved for workers on the factory floor. Godfrey then said he had been at home, but this was not corroborated by his mother, who thought he was still in his job.

After three hours of questioning he told a story Sergeant Ewbank believed. He had left home at the usual time, not daring to tell his mother he had been sacked, wandered around town, had a cup of coffee, put his name down at the Job Center, gone up on to Burley Common, and there seen a body by the side of the road. The time, he thought, was eleven thirty or a little earlier. What he had thought a sleeping or drunken figure turned out to be a dead one, and proved an irresistible temptation. He dragged the body to the shallow ditch where it had been found, began to search it for money, but panicked when two or three cars went by, afraid that one would stop and question him. He got to his heels and ran.

"He's telling the truth," Ewbank said. "We've seen him before, of course, and he wouldn't say boo to a goose, let alone attack anybody. Doesn't take us much further."

"A little way," Craxton said. "It narrows the time. We know now it must have been between ten and eleven thirty, almost certainly near eleven thirty because cars do go up the lane, and one would surely have stopped if they saw a body lying beside the road."

"So maybe it happened just a few minutes before Godfrey came on the scene."

"Or the murder took place earlier somewhere else altogether, or in a car. Certainly it didn't take place in Lover's Lane. It's a car we're looking for, going up the lane at some time near to eleven thirty."

Three car drivers came forward in response to another radio appeal. All were quickly cleared.

PART THREE

The Hit Man

1

A week later she had lunch with Debbie. Neither she nor Victor had made any reference to the photographs, or what had been said after she found them. Victor was jaunty, considerate, occasionally amusing, apparently affectionate—as he had always been or seemed, she supposed. On her side, she tried to play a similar responsive role, of the wife who accepted her husband's peccadilloes were a thing of the past and was prepared to forgive if not forget them. She wondered sometimes why she was doing just what he would have wished, and realized she lacked the heart for any decisive action after what she had no doubt was the end of her affair with Billy. Victor disgusted her, but what would have been the point of leaving a man who now treated her with the courtesy of a stranger, when she had nowhere to go, nobody to love? She knew now that she had never been in love before and felt she had thrown away the only thing that gave her life any meaning. When the telephone rang she answered it with nerves jangling and hand shaking, but it was never the call she hoped for. Patty, who came Derek-accompanied, said she looked peaky.

119

"You're sickening for something, shouldn't be surprised. Lots of this summer flu about, Carl had it." Judith asked if he needed nursing, and Patty laughed. "Dunno, if he did he was unlucky. Rocky's back, Carl had to move out, didn't like it. Been to Amsterdam, Rocky, brought this back for me." *This* was a gold necklace, in appearance similar to those in the window of Wyfleet jewellers. "Fourteen carat, Rocky got it cheap. Brought something for Derek too. Derek, show what Rocky got for you."

Derek, who sat with them at the kitchen table eating a doughnut, produced a clown who raised his hat and did somersaults when wound up. Judith asked if he liked it.

"Orright, I'spose, I wanted Action Powered Big Kat." Judith said they probably didn't have them in Holland. "Course they have, they got them everywhere."

"Derek, I'll take it away."

"Don't care."

"And I'll tell Carl, he'll come 'round and give you one 'round the earhole." Derek made a sneering face, went off to watch television. Judith asked where Carl had gone. "Dunno, he kips down anywhere, got lots of places. I get a bit sick of him hanging round all the time saying he's skint, I mean we'd all be skint if we went around backing the wrong dogs, spending other people's money. Borrowing he calls it, Rocky says he'd give it to you if he had it, only he never does have it. He's soft, Rocky is. Mind you, Carl's got a way with him."

Questions would be foolish, but she could not resist them. "When Rocky goes away again Carl will come back?"

"Less he's won on the dogs or found some mug he can take money off at snooker. But yeah, he wants to come back he'll come back."

"And you say you're sick of him, but if he comes back you'd sleep with him?"

From under the frizz of hair that Patty was now wearing low down over her forehead, the eyes of a small surprised animal peered at her. "Course I would, I mean you got to, no

120

question. Anyway, told you Carl's got a way with him, he's like, what you call it, romantic. Tough too. The Fighting Foreigners, that group I told you he was in, they used to get in fights, not just doing it for the show. But he can be nice, Carl, you know, talk you into doing what he wants, kind of an actor, well, he used to be, I told you. And tough. He's been inside for GBH, Carl." She spoke as if grievous bodily harm was an award for merit. "Course, Rocky's not like that, Rocky's sweet. Dunno which I like best really. Carl's exciting, I do get pissed off with him though." She coloured, said, "Excuse me, sorry," got up from the table and switched on the vacuum cleaner. You can hear the words any evening on TV, Judith thought, did Patty think of her as a maiden aunt who'd be shocked by them? Probably she did. Or perhaps she felt it was wrong to use such a phrase when talking to her employer? Perhaps. Anyway, there was Patty, a pleasant girl, a good mother, not lazy or sluttish, yet the gap between her way of thinking and talking and Judith's was too great to be bridged.

On the way to lunch with Debbie, she turned off the road into town and entered the Estate. It had been built by the Council several years earlier, at a time when the revulsion from tower blocks was at its most intense. There were no tower blocks in Wyfleet, but the surge of media publicity saying that the true-born Englishman was only happy living in his own house with his own patch of grass and his own front gate had its effect on the Council. There were, accordingly, no flats on the Estate but a multitude of little red brick houses which differed only in minor details, on streets all named after flowers. The whole made up a kind of maze from which, Judith found, it was not easy to escape. Entry into it was simple enough. She passed a board saying "Orchard Estate," with a layout beneath it to which, she later realized she should have paid attention, and went down Geranium Street which branched out in three directions named Rose, Lupin, and Daffodil. She chose Daffodil, which divided into Dahlia and

Larkspur, went off Larkspur into Magnolia, and at the end of Magnolia was confronted with Peony and Aster. Turning into Aster, she came back to Lupin, but when she went down Lupin in search of Geranium or Daffodil, both seemed to have vanished.

The houses were all of two stories in blocks varying from six to ten in size, each with its front gate and tiny garden. No provision had been made for garages, and the streets were lined with parked cars, most of them between five and twenty years old, Fords, Austins, Vauxhalls and Volkswagens interspersed with beat-up Buicks, Jaguars, and cars she had not seen on the roads for years, like ACs, Morgans, and a Singer that must have been built forty years ago. The most obvious sign of activity on the Estate was little knots of men gathered round cars with their bonnets up, peering at the engines, doing something or other with spanners, revving up, changing tires, even in one case apparently changing a numberplate. She had no idea of Billy's address, but Patty lived in Hyacinth Street and she stopped beside four youths looking at the engine of an old Triumph, wound down her window, and asked how she got to Hyacinth Street. One of them, a tow-haired boy of perhaps sixteen, approached her grinning. He gabbled something she didn't understand, and she said, "I'm afraid I didn't quite hear you."

He turned back to his mates and said, "She's afraaaid she din't quaaate hyar me, oh deeear ay em sawry." In the same caricatured version of her voice he said, "Ay saaid whay not come into the heeause end ay'll give yeeou one." His friends exploded into laughter. She put the car into gear and shot away, braking sharply to avoid a woman crossing the road with a loaded basket in either hand. Judith stopped, and asked the way to Hyacinth Street.

"You should be more bleeding careful."

"I'm sorry."

"Left at the end, left again at the T junction, second right off Amaranth, down Orchid and it's second left." She turned into her gate before Judith could say thanks or ask for something more specific.

Hyacinth, when she found it, was like all the other streets. What had she expected? She cruised slowly down it looking from side to side, hoping to see Patty or Derek, but the houses turned blank faces to her. When at last she escaped from the Estate, after going down two or three streets that proved to be dead ends, petering out into large turning circles for cars, she found herself taking deep breaths as if exhausted after a long run. The Estate showed no particular signs of deprivation, there was nothing unusual about it except for the number of parked cars, yet something about those blocks of houses in streets whose appearance belied the names they had been given, seemed to her frightening. If the names were all removed one night, how would one tell Larkspur from Peony, Magnolia from Hyacinth?

She was late at Luigi's. Debbie looked at her critically and asked what was up. She explained she had driven round the Estate.

"What for? You must be crazy."

"I just felt like having a look at it, and I got lost. Well, sort of lost."

"But the Estate, I mean it's the last place anyone in their senses would want to look at, it was only put up like that because a lot of people did nicely out of it." She looked disconcerted for a moment, changed conversational course. "You know what, you look like a nice proper Wyfleet housewife, and you're married to a nice Wyfleet professional man or whatever you call it, but underneath you're just a little bit crazy. That's why I like you."

She did not reply, but when they had ordered she said, "Is that what you think about Victor and me, that we're nice ordinary people?"

"Why, yes. Aren't you?" Her dark eyes were sharp.

"And what you said about getting the urge every six months or so and doing something about it, you meant that?"

123

"Yes, darling. But don't expect to hear the lurid details."

"I don't, but—it's all a game to you, is that right?"

"Healthy exercise, none better." Her fine small white teeth showed. "Do I feel a confession on the way? No names, I don't want to hear them, but would I be right in thinking my dear proper friend Judith is having a *fling*?"

"Perhaps. I didn't want to talk about that, but—" What was it? Her mind became fixed on colours, the chaste pink and grey of the little mock-Tiffany lamp that shed a faint light on their table, the red and white check cloth, the pink of Debbie's prawn cocktail, the green skin of her own avocado.

"If you don't want to talk, why say anything?" The sharp words were belied by the grin that followed them. "Funny, isn't it? I do some things I shouldn't, but up here is hard as a nut." She tapped her head. "I've got my head screwed on the right way as dad used to say. You now, there you are all buttoned up, but inside I guess everything's churning round and round. Isn't that so, has doctor Debbie got it right? All right, darling, I won't pry, I'll only say do what you like but don't do anything silly. You've got a good marriage, take care you don't muck it up. What's so funny?"

She was laughing, laughing helplessly, because Debbie's words were so like what Annabel the novelist had said to her, and were so far from reality. "It's just that somebody, somebody else said that to me. And you see, it's not true."

"Victor's been playing around?"

How should she reply to that? Just as she had not wanted to spell out any details about Billy or to mention his name, so now she found herself unable to say anything more about Victor than that, yes, she supposed you could call it playing around.

"You only suppose? It either is or isn't, surely. You certainly do raise a girl's curiosity. You want me to tell you how to carry on an affair in five easy lessons, is that it? Well, it depends on the other party, but if it's someone we know and I have to think it is, you should both of you be *very* careful . . . And

Debbie went on with what was no doubt sensible advice about avoiding letters and telephone calls, making arrangements at each meeting about the next one, but there was nothing she wanted to hear so she broke in to ask what Debbie herself had done in the past, was perhaps doing now, did she always follow her own advice? As she asked this, she was aware of pain in her fingers and saw one hand was gripping the other so tightly that the engagement ring Victor had given her was hurting her other hand.

"Darling, you're very *fraught*, but all right, if you want to know, with me it's nothing serious, just a kind of itch. A couple of months ago we were at the Bradens', a big dinner party. He's a very attractive man, Clive, don't you think? Anyway, I've always thought so, and I know he feels the same way, though of course for men it's different. Anyway, I caught Clive's eye, he knew what I was saying or rather not saying, followed me out, took me to a bedroom, and twenty minutes later I was back at the party feeling much better."

"I couldn't do anything like that."

"I'm sure you couldn't, so what's the use of me talking? Just be careful, is all. I think we ought to stop talking about this, it seems to be making you more fraught, not less. Anyway, I've got something to say, which is why I said let's have lunch. And cross my heart, I don't know what it's all about, so no good asking, but you know that policeman Craxton."

"I was at school with him when we were children, that's all."

"Anyway you know him. And he said something or other to you about Victor getting into trouble."

"No. He said there was some sort of trouble likely, and I should tell Victor to keep his nose clean. Trouble about Burley Common, I think. That was all. I told Victor, he didn't seem to know what I meant."

"No more do I. But Victor must have said something to Johnny, and Johnny wants you to find out."

She stared at Debbie, incredulous. "You mean, ask him?"

125

"I suppose so."

"I shouldn't think of it. And anyway, of course he wouldn't tell me."

"He isn't—?"

For a moment she didn't understand. Then she burst out laughing. "Am I having an affair with him? No, absolutely not. Cups of tea in the Safeway café, that's all."

"All right, you may not fancy him, but Johnny thinks he must fancy you, otherwise why should he have been dropping hints. Unless of course he was trying to set alarm bells ringing, which also occurred to Johnny. He's like me, got his head screwed on the right way." Her smile was perfunctory. "And Johnny wants to know which it is. Whether the cops think they're on to something, or just trying to muddy the water and stop Burley Common from coming off."

"Why would they do that?"

"Don't ask me, I'm only repeating what my master told me."

They were at the coffee stage. Judith put in more sugar than she intended. "You can tell Johnny I hardly know Craxton, and anyway I wouldn't dream of trying to worm information out of him."

Debbie spread her hands. "Don't shoot the messenger. You'd still feel the same, even if there was trouble ahead for Victor?"

"About young Nethersole?"

"I don't know, I told you I don't know what any of this is about."

"I'd still feel the same."

2

The two telephone calls came on the following day, in the morning, within half an hour of each other. The first surprised, the second delighted her.

"Jack Craxton, remember me?" She would have known the voice by the local burr, which was more noticeable on the telephone. "You sound surprised."

"I am."

"Fair enough. I rang to ask you to have lunch with me one day. Professional, two or three things I'd like to talk to you about. Personal as well though, I told you that. Say yes, you won't be sorry."

Although she had told Debbie she wouldn't dream of trying to get information out of Craxton there seemed no reason why she shouldn't say yes to lunch, and she did. She added that he sounded very businesslike.

"That's professional me. But personal me will be glad to see you. I know you've got wheels, so can we say the Red Dragon at Lineham if that's okay for you. I'll book a table. One o'clock suit you? Fine, I'll look forward to it."

She thought, oddly enough so shall I. When the telephone rang again ten minutes later, she thought he wanted to change the time or the place and was ready to say he should know his own mind, but the voice that said "It's me," was not Craxton's. The sound of the voice, those two words, made her feel so weak she had to put down the telephone on the table beside her chair. The voice went on. "Look, sorry about it, you said I shouldn't, can you talk, hello." That last *hello* had a desperate sound to it.

"Hello, yes, I'm here and it's all right. I was surprised, that's all."

"Just, better not on the blower, wanted to see you. That okay?" She said yes. "Soon as you like, usual place, how about this afternoon, half two?"

She said yes again. When she put down the telephone she could have cried with joy. It seemed to her a miracle that she was seeing him again. The reason, whatever it might be, was unimportant. And the miracle extended to the Marvin, which she saw with different eyes as she turned into the side street and went through the narrow entrance into the yard where cars had to be parked alongside bits of motorbikes, old tires and black plastic bags full of rubbish. One other car was parked there, a Vauxhall Astra with one wing battered and the bonnet badly dented. She had seen a dozen cars in similar condition during her tour of the Estate, yet she knew instinctively that Billy had come in this one and would be waiting for her. She gave the merest glance at the register to see "Mr. and Mrs. Smith" written there in a rounded careful schoolboy's hand, savoured the worn carpet and the peeling brown paint of the stairs, opened the door and almost ran into his arms.

When they embraced it was as if she was holding him and feeling the warmth of his body for the first time. And not only feeling, but smelling. As they undressed without speaking, she smelt his body as she had not done before, a smell that was milky and sweet almost as if he were a child. She had the sensation of touching a child as she caressed the youthful innocence of his neck, stroked his arms and murmured inadequate words. Afterwards she held his hand and said, "Wonderful, wonderful, I thought I'd lost you."

"Fantastic, I told you already, just fantastic."

There was a momentary twinge as she thought of other women to whom he might have used the word. Then she banished it and said she felt about him as if he were a little boy. He laughed, said pretty big little boy, then sensed that was perhaps not what she wanted to hear. "I don't think that way, just a man and a woman innit, that's all." She asked if he had come in the Astra and he said yes, borrowed it from a mate.

"I've seen some like it on the Estate. I went down there hoping to see you, tell you I was sorry."

"Shouldn'ta gone down there, can be dodgy, specially at night."

"It was in the morning, so that was all right. I wanted to say I'd been silly, forget it, but of course I didn't know where you lived, and I got lost because all the streets looked the same."

"Too right they do. What I wanted, was about what you said, I mean." He lighted a cigarette, got up, began to walk about the room. "I mean, see, I may've found somebody, do what, you know, what we talked about."

Just as she had known he would be here waiting, so it seemed to her that she had known it was inevitable he should find a way of ensuring they spent the rest of their lives together, somewhere away from Wyfleet and perhaps out of England, in Canada or California or wherever he wanted to be. She listened, but part of her also dreamed, as he told her about the seaman he had met in a pub who was spending the money from his last trip on a girl he knew who lived on the Estate. She did not really follow all that he said in the ragged jumbled slipshod phrases that seemed to curl round and be repeated with a number of names, none of them English, Anders and Willem and somebody who seemed to be named

Hammer, José and Ricardo and the Jewboy. It was not just one pub they had been in but two or three, and then there had been some card game in the Jewboy's house. There was something about a tart he had been with.

"Who?" she said. "Who was with this—did you say her name was Louise?"

"Louisa. I just told you, it was Willem." He put on shirt and shorts and now stood almost glaring down at her as she sat on the bed. She did not want to upset him, and said she thought it was in somebody's house—she did not like to say Jewboy. He interrupted impatiently.

"It's his pad, that's all, I dunno what his name is, we all call him the Jewboy. Thing is he don't live here, don't live anywhere what I can make out. So he pulls out a wad of notes, twenties and some of 'em fifties, I says they pay well on the boats and he says there's other ways of putting a roll together, and then this tart asks what he means and he laughs and says he's a disposal expert. What's that, I says what's disposal, what do you get rid of. You know what he says, he says people."

"This is not the Jewboy?"

"For Crissake, you deaf? I told you it's Willem, what he calls hisself, I dunno it's his real name, don't matter."

She listened, loving his childish excitement but not believing what he said, or what Willem had said, about doing a job in Caracas where he was employed by an engineering firm to dispose of a man trying to get plans for a new kind of car silencer the firm made, and another in Buenos Aires for a politician who was being blackmailed because of his liking for nymphets, and a third in Hamburg for a professor of music who wanted to get rid of an old wife and marry a young mistress. The thing was, Billy said, he didn't live anywhere, not permanently. You paid him, he did the job, then he used one of his dozen passports and went underground. The police here could look all they liked for him, he wouldn't be around—

She stopped him. "But my darling, it's all talk, you don't

know he's done any of those things." He stopped walking up and down, glared at her. She said gently, mother to mistaken child, "It sounds to me as if he's just a man boasting. If he'd done these things he wouldn't talk about them."

"He didn't. It was the girl talked about them first. He only—I got it out of him." He shook his head. "That's not it, got to tell you the way it was. The two of us, we don't kid each other. When he says about the disposal bit, I says to him maybe I got a job might interest him, or might know someone'd be interested. It was then he said about the jobs he done. Maybe I shouldn't, I thought it was what you wanted."

The fire had gone out of him. He came and sat beside her on the bed. She put an arm round him and he rested his head on her shoulder. He murmured something she did not hear and asked him to repeat, and he muttered it almost sullenly.

"I want it too, being together and that. And abroad, you said we could go abroad."

"I know I did, but it's just, this doesn't seem right."

"It was you wanted it, now you don't. Okay then." He got up off the bed. The thought of losing him was unbearable.

"This Willem—that's his name?"

"One he goes by, reckon he's got half a dozen."

"You've made some arrangement with him, is that it?"

"No arrangement, said I'd let him know if you was interested. Don't mean *you*, just said might know somebody, didn't give a glimmer who it was, man or woman, nothing."

When she said she supposed it wouldn't hurt to see this Willem, he came over and hugged her, again like a child. He kissed her, with what she felt were the kisses of a repentant child to a forgiving mother. Then he checked himself, said again it was what she wanted, and he wanted it too so that they could be together. This delighted her so much that she felt prepared to promise anything, but she restrained herself, remembering that he was the rash child, she the wise mother.

But the child was not entirely rash. He said, what she was thinking, that she should meet Willem on her own and that it should be away from Wyfleet, somewhere she wouldn't meet anybody who knew her, but where? She could not take it quite seriously, it was a kind of game they were playing, and like somebody playing a game she clapped her hands when she thought of a place.

"On the front at Hastings, almost opposite the pier, a place called the Mikado café. I went there once." She had been out with Victor, they had stopped there for tea. "How will I know him?"

"I'll tell him what you look like, he'll know you. Tomorrow, half four, that all right?"

"You said he might be leaving tomorrow."

"Yeah, well." He paused. "Stuff I haven't told you." She waited. "All that, the way I met him, that was straight up. Thing is, he never stayed here, he's up in London."

She was puzzled. "So why did you tell me he was staying here?"

"Thought—I dunno why. Just, he's a pro, see, a real pro, what they call a hit man. Thought it might put you off, I told you that."

"I know what a hit man is. So how will you get in touch with him?"

"I never said any names or stuff like that, way I told you, and it's right about him not living anywhere. I got a number to call in London, talk to him on the blower, say if you wanted a meet or you'd had, you know, didn't like the idea, him being a pro."

She found the idea of meeting a professional exciting, in part because it seemed to make the whole thing more than ever a game, something she could safely plan because it would never happen. Yet at the same time the professionalism gave the idea a contradictory solidity, a sort of guarantee that if she did go ahead it would be done properly, not bungled as Foster had bungled his arrangement. When she said all right, he seemed surprised.

"You'll meet him?"

"Why not? It won't commit either of us to anything."

"I'll give him a bell then, say half four tomorrow, okay?" She said yes. "If you don't hear anything it's on. If he says no or puts it off I'll call you, put the phone down as soon as you or anybody picks it up, okay?" She said okay. "Something else I oughta tell you, what he said to me. It'll cost."

She hardly paid attention to that. "This means I shan't see you tomorrow."

"I dunno we oughta meet, not till it's done. Anyone gets a line on us—" She protested so vehemently that he checked himself, said he supposed if they were careful it would be all right, they would meet here at the Marvin on Thursday afternoon.

It was not until after they had parted that she remembered he had not told her the name of the road he lived in. Not that it mattered, because if the pro did a good job Billy wouldn't live there much longer.

3

There was no telephone call. Before driving to Hastings, she read some further details of the Foster case. After the failure of the wired-up meeting, Doorlock had introduced Foster to a "professional killer" who was in fact an undercover policeman. Elaborate plans were made for shooting Mrs. Foster with a long-range rifle with telescopic sights. Foster had been arrested when he went to pay the first installment of cash. From the questions asked by Foster's counsel it seemed clear he was going to say the telescopic rifle was a police invention, and that Foster was sticking to his story of wanting his wife taught a lesson, but not a fatal one.

On the drive to Hastings, and then as she parked the car a quarter of a mile away from the meeting place and walked along the front towards the café, her mind was busy with what she might learn from Foster's débâcle. One lesson was the foolishness of involving more people than absolutely necessary. In this case there was Billy, who could be relied on not to talk, and the two principals, Willem and herself. The idea that Willem could be a police spy was ludicrously unlikely.

But Foster had also been stupid in agreeing to something that was evidently murder. When one partner in a marriage dies violently the other is the obvious suspect. No doubt Foster had arranged to be away when the event occurred, but his plan was flawed from the beginning.

At these thoughts, the calculating solemnity of them, the *seriousness* with which she contemplated the whole thing, she could have burst out laughing, because it was still only a game. All options are still open, she thought, if I don't believe in this Willem, don't trust him, don't like him, I shall say thank you and goodbye and I shall be happy to pay your first class train fare back to London. It is all as much a game as those letters I used to hope Victor would ask me to open, as much a game as the one I played with Billy before the vital words were spoken: "Be gentle." Even now what she did with Billy was a game, a game of mother and child. It was not like the reality of the photographs. Yet something, another voice within her, said there was little difference between what went on in the photographs and what she did with Billy. At that thought she could have screamed, and did actually say out loud: "*Not* the same, Billy and I love each other." She thumped the steering wheel to make the point, then admonished herself: "Judith Lassiter, don't be stupid."

She reached the café to find it was not called the Mikado but the TeasReady. She walked a little way past it to make sure. There was a café called Lesley's and a small restaurant named the Open Door, but no Mikado. She opened the door, which made a bell tinkle, and asked the adenoidal young waitress if this had once been the Mikado. The girl gaped at her, called out to somebody at the back, and a stately woman appeared and said yes, this had been the Mikado, but she had taken it over three years ago and changed the name. "People seem to prefer it. TeasReady is rather clever, don't you think? And tea *is* ready, at any time you like."

Judith realized that she had broken her own rule by calling attention to herself. She said she was waiting for a friend, and sat in one of the high-backed cubicles with benches on either side. She remembered them, and indeed had remembered the Mikado because Victor had said the cubicles would be ideal for people who wanted to meet privately. Would Willem find it? To have given him the wrong name was a bad start, but she could say she had been testing him deliberately. If he came.

She had been waiting no more than five minutes when the bell tinkled. A man came in, a man on his own. She looked round the side of the cubicle, he saw her, slid into the bench opposite her, said "Hallo."

He was not what she had been expecting. There was no reason why she should have "expected" anything in particular, but she had thought of the hit man as somebody in his middle twenties, big and obviously tough. The man opposite was perhaps forty years old, of medium size and height with a thin, clever face. He wore on this warm day a grey sweater over a grubby open-neck shirt, corduroy trousers and rather dirty trainers. He looked like a badly paid school-teacher taking a day's holiday by the sea.

It occurred to her that perhaps this was not Willem, but just a man trying to pick her up. She said she was expecting to meet somebody. His brief smile, with a downturn of the whole mouth, made him look so vicious that she changed her mind about his harmlessness.

"You expect me, Willem. You were very careful." She looked at him, momentarily bewildered. "You give me the wrong name for this place, just setting me a little problem, yes?" He gave her the smile again before saying, "I solved it." His English was perfect, although the stresses were sometimes unusual. He emphasized the second syllable of the "problem."

She began to explain, but he checked her by raising his hand. "Doesn't matter." The adenoidal waitress appeared, and she was about to order simply a pot of tea for two, but he checked her again, "You have a toasted teacake?"

She said in a sing-song voice: "Toasted teacake, pastries, welsh rarebit, poached egg on welsh rarebit, Devonshire cream tea—"

He stopped her. "Devonshire cream tea. And toasted tea-cake. Nothing for you?" She shook her head. When the girl had gone he said, "We are a couple having tea, yes? If you order food they like it. Now, our friend tells me you have a little difficulty."

"Our friend? Oh yes, of course."

"He described you well. Unmistakably." He lingered over each syllable. "You have brought a photograph?"

"A photograph?"

"Of the subject. I shall need one. And of course a name. An address. Also some details of habits. If the subject has a routine, then I can make plans accordingly. Am I going too fast for you? I think perhaps so, I apologize. Perhaps it would be better if you talk to me, instead of me to you. You tell me what is in your mind, I promise not to speak. My mouth will be filled with toasted teacake. Here it comes, and the scones, and the cream." He bestowed the smile on the waitress, who seemed to find nothing unusual in it, and smiled back. Judith poured tea for them both. She found it difficult to begin. He bit into the teacake.

"I find it hard to—" He merely nodded, and waited. What was it Foster had said? That he was bored with his wife, and wished something would happen to her? She said haltingly, "I don't want to talk about the reasons."

Through a mouthful of teacake he said, "Not my business."

"It's somebody I want to—disappear." Another nod. She had said it, the secret was out, he remained unshocked. But of course he was unshocked, he was a professional. She went on more easily.

"You'll want the name as well, no point trying to hide it's my husband. And I can let you have a photograph. This is something you know about, you've done it before. That's right, isn't it?"

He gave her the smile. "Quite right."

"There's one thing that's specially important, no I mean essential. It must happen so that there is no suspicion."

He finished the teacake, and wiped his mouth before answering. "Of you? That is what would happen, is it? Suspicion of you?"

"Yes. Quite a lot of money would come to me."

"A car accident perhaps? If he goes out for walks, takes the dog for an evening run, a hit and run driver? A burglary, he interrupts it, is hit too hard? Perhaps he takes drugs or drinks heavily? He takes too much to drink, too strong a sleeping pill, passes out, starts a fire when a cigarette drops from his fingers. Of course you have an engagement that evening. Cream before jam, you think? I am never sure." He loaded the scone with cream, added jam. "Why are you shaking your head?"

"We have no dog. He doesn't take drugs or sleeping pills, drinks moderately, never goes for evening walks."

"Only suggestions. We'll think of something else. This cream is ex-cell-ent." He licked a little off the corner of his mouth. "I told you, I must know details of his habits. Or perhaps you have a suggestion."

You are the expert, she thought resentfully, it's for you to come up with the solution. She said she would let him have a photograph, and try to give some details of habits, although beyond the fact that he left for the office at a regular time and returned punctually on most days around six o'clock, she could think of none.

"He plays golf perhaps, belongs to a club? No? Never mind. You make for me a list of his movements each day, I shall find something." When she asked if she should send them to an address he shook his head. "No addresses. We meet again, you bring the photograph, the details."

"But that means I have to trust you, you don't trust me."

He gave her the smile. "I give you away, what does it matter to you? You deny everything. You give me away, I have a reputation. I am a professional, not an amateur. Forty-eight hours after the work is finished I shall be in Buenos Aires, I don't mind then what you say. You understand?" She said she understood. "So we meet again in this ex-cell-ent teashop." He glanced at his clean plate. "We have not discussed a figure. Ten."

"Ten what? I don't understand."

"Ten grand is the figure, half down, the rest when the affair is brought to a satisfactory conclusion."

She said incredulously, "Ten thousand pounds, that's ridiculous." She was conscious of her raised voice, and lowered it as she repeated, "Ridiculous." She felt like saying that Foster's man had asked only a hundred. But then of course Foster's man had been a nark.

"If you really want the job done, that is the figure. But perhaps you don't."

"I'm beginning to think that too." She got up and walked out, leaving him in the cubicle, his mouth slightly open in surprise. She was halfway back to Wyfleet when she remembered she had left him to pay the bill.

4

You were a sort of dream figure to me," Jack Craxton said. "My dad was a copper, never made sergeant, not too bright though that's not how I thought about him when I was a kid. I wanted to wear a uniform like his the way some kids want to be sailors or bus conductors. Think they want to, anyway. There was a row of cottages down the lane, quarter of a mile past the school, Grantley's Cottages they were called after the man who put 'em up. No reason why you should remember them, two up, two down, plus a sort of wooden extension with bath and toilet that was so draughty you felt colder when you got out of the bath than when you went in. Four kids, two boys and two girls, all in one room, just a curtain between us my ma rigged up, I was the eldest. A bit different from Three Gables. I used to fantasize about you, got your own room, breakfast brought up to you, maid to get you dressed, polish your shoes, no wonder you always looked happy. Don't suppose it was quite like that."

"It certainly wasn't. There was a nanny who looked after me, a sort of combined nanny and housekeeper because my mother was pretty hopeless at anything to do with household things, but she was quite strict. I cleaned my own shoes."

"You can guess my dreams or fantasies or whatever you call 'em never went as far as taking you to lunch here." They sat in the bar of the hotel, the walls of which were done out in different tartans, with the name of each clan above them. She considered him, a hard-faced man who was at that moment looking shyly into his glass of the local bitter, and wondered what he would say if she told him that yesterday she had been talking to a hit man about ways in which he might dispose of her husband. Unreal, she thought, I can't have been serious. But still, it seemed no more unreal than sitting in a bar listening to a policeman talk about his childhood. It's all fantasy, she thought, the whole of life is unreal. She felt a strong impulse to tell him about Victor and the photographs, in the hope that he would understand her need to break free, and that since a divorce was not possible this must be done in the most decisive way of all. But she knew she must say nothing of the sort, and told him instead of the longing for romance that made her write letters to herself. He raised his thick eyebrows.

"And he never did? I would have done, you can be certain, I might even have opened them without telling you. And you really did that, wrote letters to yourself?"

"Wasn't it silly? But I get, I don't know what you'd call it, impulses, and then I do funny things. Sometimes."

"Let's go in to lunch." While they ate steak and drank rough red wine he talked easily, amusingly, about how pleased his father had been when he put on the uniform, and how proud when his son was the first in his intake to be made up to sergeant. Still prouder, she suggested, now he was chief inspector. He shook his head.

"Dad died five years ago."

"I'm sorry."

"Don't be. He had a heart attack, they made him take retirement, he hated it, drank himself to death. Anyway he didn't take much to policemen in plain clothes, said most of 'em were rogues and vagabonds. I think sometimes he wasn't far out."

"But you're not? A rogue or vagabond?"

"I'm your honest copper. Which isn't always easy. You're in a closed group, a tight little society, got its own language, its own code. Some things you do, some you don't. Same applies to any closed group, teachers, doctors, lawyers. Even families."

"Are you telling me something, warning me about something?"

"I've said it already, and I hope you passed it on. If there are papers and stuff around that would be bad news, they should go in the shredder. Plain enough?" She said nothing. "I'm saying things you don't say in my closed group, but you're still a kind of dream figure to me, and I reckon you make exceptions." His bold dark eyes made her shiver in a different way from the smile of the hit man, with sexual expectation, not fear. "Something off beam about you, you know that? You say yes and no and perhaps, but half the time I have the feeling you're somewhere else. Mostly I like my women simple and straightforward—"

"Like Verna Upwood you mean? The one you said was wood from the neck up?"

"Not like Verna Upwood."

"And in any case, I'm not your woman."

"Sorry about that. I wish you were. But have you understood what I've been telling you?

"I don't think so, no. You see, I just don't understand what's going on."

They walked out of the pub into the warm air. He caught hold of her arm. "Here it is, then. Tell him the balloon's going up, very soon. I don't want my dream figure to go up with it." He swung her around, kissed her hard on lips that remained closed, turned his back on her, walked to his car. She ran her tongue over her lips and tasted beer.

5

Victor returned home later than usual that evening, and she was asleep. In the morning she told him she had lunched with Craxton.

"Why should he ask you to lunch?"

"Because he likes me. Do you think that's impossible? You said I shouldn't talk to him, Debbie told me Johnny was keen for me to see him again, find out what he knew. So when he invited me to lunch I said yes."

"All right. What did he say?"

"That the balloon would go up very soon. He was kind enough to say he didn't want me to go up with it."

"Nothing else?"

"Yes. He said you should put any papers that might cause trouble in the shredder. He didn't say anything about photographs, but I expect he'd include them."

"It's talk, that's all. Trying to frighten people." His fingers went to his bow tie, came away without touching it.

"It didn't sound like that. Anyway, that's what he said to me, and now I've passed it on."

He came round to her smiling, took her hand, kissed it. "I'm sorry. Things are a bit tense just now. I believe Craxton's carrying on a war of nerves. Johnny—well, he thinks there's something more to it."

"He's found out about Nethersole?"

"Perhaps." His lips touched her cheek. "I shan't be late tonight."

When he had gone she sat looking at herself for some minutes in the bedroom glass, then went out into the garden, gazed over the fields towards the sea, then turned and considered the house, the deck and the stilts supporting it, the roof's glittering green. I hate it all, she thought, the house, my life, most of all Victor. I must be free of him, I won't let him drag up the past, I won't let his sneering barrister ask about Billy, how often and did I enjoy it and how many others have there been and then, what about Hubert, we've heard him say you threw yourself at him and almost forced him to make love to you, were you really so shocked by those photographs, Mrs. Lassiter, after all you're a sexually experienced woman. . . .

She cried out something, ran back to the house, put her hands over her eyes. The need for Billy's presence and his arms round her made her whole body ache. She went back into the bedroom, lay on the bed, took a pillow in her arms, closed her eyes, crooned loving words to it. Off beam, that's the trouble with me, she thought, I'm off beam. She put another pillow between her legs and lay there, not sleeping yet not wholly awake, her mind filled with images of Billy, the whiteness of his body and its milky childish smell, the silky hair on his arms, the gentleness with which he made love. She saw herself going to Wyfleet Travel and smiling at the girl as she asked the cost of a flight to Los Angeles. You want the return fare? the girl asked, and looked surprised when she said no, one way. What, you're not coming back then? No, we're emigrating, yes, two people, my friend and I are leaving England for good.

She opened her eyes, looked round the bedroom, sat up,

pushed away the pillows. Stupid, stupid, she thought, it's all nonsense. She had looked at the balance of the personal account Victor had insisted she should have soon after their marriage. It stood at fifteen hundred pounds, with another six thousand in a deposit account. How long would that last, in California or anywhere else? It was nonsense, silly dreaming. And what did she know about Billy? Had he forgotten to tell her where he lived, or was there some reason why he didn't want her to know it, perhaps he lived with a girl his own age and his mother was a fiction.

The telephone rang. Billy, she thought, it must be Billy, I pray it's Billy. Yet she hardly believed it when she heard his voice.

"Okay to talk? Hear it didn't go right, your meet." She said she didn't like Willem, and what he asked was out of the question.

"Yeah, well. Think we should talk. Two thirty, usual place?" The need to be firm, not give way, robbed her of speech. He said questioningly, "That okay?"

The next words seemed the most difficult she had ever spoken. "I want to come to your house, Billy. I don't even know the address."

Silence. Then he said. "Not a good idea. You been down the Estate once, seen what it's like." She said it was what she wanted, she wanted to see where he lived. Another silence. "Okay, eighteen Primula. But you got to listen, do what I say, okay? My mum thinks I'm still with Ron, right, don't know about my bit of bother. So you betta be a client, called 'cause I got the time wrong, didn't turn up when I shoulda done, okay? Then I say sorry forget, we go off together. Got it straight?"

She said she had it straight. Driving down to the Estate she felt joy, relief and guilt, joy at the thought of seeing him again, relief at proof that he really did live with his mother, guilt that she had doubted him. This time she looked at the board by the entrance, and found Primula Street without difficulty.

It was shorter than some, and there were fewer clapped-out cars lining the curbs, so that she found a parking space. Number eighteen had the usual small patch of grass in front, but was neater than most, and there was a flower border. The flowers, she saw, were primulas. She pressed a plastic bell push.

The woman who opened the door looked in her forties or older. She was an older Billy, one battered by life so that her forehead was lined and there were dark hollows under her eyes. Yet there was an air of determination about her that Billy lacked. She looked as if she was expecting life to give her a few more one-twos, but would always come up fighting. Judith haltingly explained that she had been expecting Billy to call on her, there had been perhaps some misunderstanding.

"I'm his mother. Come in."

She entered a crowded front room which contained a large TV set, a three piece suite, a carpet in violent reds and blues, and on the mantlepiece several small plastic figures of a variety of dogs ranging from a corgi and a dachshund to a bulldog and a Great Dane. Mrs. Gay closed the door.

"Billy's just popped out to see a friend, he'll be back in a few minutes, but I'm pleased to have the chance of a chat." Was Mrs. Gay somehow aware of their relationship? The next words undeceived her.

"He'll be ever so sorry, I know he will, there's been a mix-up, he's usually so careful. But I just wanted to ask you if you thought he could make a go of this driving he's doing for Ron Hinks. Would you say you were satisfied with his, I suppose you'd call it instruction, though it seems funny to me, Billy instructing anybody." She had the unaccented speech of southern England, without the deliberate slovenliness of her son's slipping together of words. Judith said he was very good.

"I'm very pleased you say that, Mrs.—"

"Lassiter."

"Very pleased. Billy's a good boy, just a bit forgetful at times, like he's been about this appointment with you, I hope you feel you can overlook it, not tell Ron Hinks. That's good of you. I'll tell you Billy's trouble, he finds it hard to settle to anything, but then a lot do nowadays. Do you have children, Mrs. Lassiter? You don't? Billy's my only one, and he's been a blessing but a handful too. The teachers used to say he was bright but had no application, I said to them he's able to apply himself when it's something he likes, anything to do with cars and machinery, just not one for book learning, that's all. And then he didn't get on with his father, in my opinion that held him back. Mind you, I suppose you'd say it was six of one and half a dozen of the other, Billy played him up something dreadful at times, ever so cheeky and his dad, he liked a glass or two and when he'd taken drink he was on what you'd call a short fuse, but he was a good man in many ways. I'd never have left him but for Billy. Spare the rod and spoil the child, I know that's what they say, but when he started knocking Billy about I thought to myself this won't do, this has got to stop. Can I get you a cup of tea, Mrs. Lassiter?"

She said no thank you and regretted it, for Mrs. Gay nodded and resumed her remorseless discourse. Billy may have resembled his mother in appearance, but her verbal flow had in him been choked off at the tap.

"So I talked to Robbie but might as well have saved my breath, talk to me he says why don't you talk to that son of yours and tell him when his father says do something he's got to do it, you take his side Robbie says and I told him I take nobody's side, just won't see my son knocked about. Then something unfortunate happens. He's easily led, you see, Billy, and I've always said what happened wasn't his doing, it was one or two he got in with, I don't believe he was even there in person as you might call it—"

"What happened, Mrs. Gay?"

"Some youths set on Robbie and put him in hospital. I don't care what anybody says, I don't believe Billy had any hand in it, but Robbie thought he had, it's him or me he says, I won't have him under my roof. So there you are."

The front door opened and closed. Billy appeared, breathless, looked surprised then penitent as Judith went into the speech she had been given. Mrs. Gay broke in.

"We've been having a nice chat all about you, Mrs. Lassiter and me, and she just said she won't say anything about you forgetting the appointment. And I told her what a good boy you are and she said she's satisfied with you as an instructor, though don't you get big-headed about it mind."

Billy ignored his mother, muttered something about being sorry and said, "Let's go." When they were outside the Estate he breathed deeply.

"All right, you got what you came for, seen my mum, know what she's like, satisfied?"

She had to restrain herself from tears. "Billy, I'm sorry. It was just not knowing where you lived, it seemed so odd. Your mother talks a lot, but I liked her. She worships you, you must know that."

"She gets on my wick." Then he said, "Dunno what she said but yeah, she's been good to me, it's just that . . ." He let the sentence trail away.

"Did you leave me alone with her deliberately, so that she'd talk to me?"

"You think I'd do that?"

"From what she told me it sounds as if you might do anything."

"Did she say that?" He began to whistle, then said, "Had to go out, give a hand to a mate of mine, one who lent me the banger."

"What sort of hand?"

"Christ, you're as nosy as my mum. Not your business. Where we going?"

"To our hotel. Unless you've got another idea."

"Can't think of a better one."

The Marvin's reception desk was empty, the onion and disinfectant smell stronger than usual. Billy banged the bell twice before the toupeed ancient appeared. He looked at them with rheumy eyes, said their usual room was taken, all the rooms were taken. She was ready to accept this and turned away, but Billy leaned across the desk and said, "Come again, Jack."

"Not Jack, Basil."

"Basil, okay, can't be all the rooms in this fleapit are taken, or why are those keys hanging up?"

"Coming later, all booked up, a party."

Billy turned to her, said in a low voice, "You got ten, ten or two fives." She stared at him and he repeated impatiently, "Ten or two fives." She fumbled in her bag, found two five pound notes. Billy thrust them across the counter, said, "No change." In the past they had paid six pounds for the use of the room. The ancient contemplated the notes for a moment, wiped his eyes, turned to where the keys hung and took down the one marked "6."

When they were in the room she said, "Does everyone now do everything for money?"

"Not everything." He embraced her, enclosed her, she knew a pleasure that lay not merely in the act but in everything surrounding it. The smell of his body was part of it, but so was the smell of onions and disinfectant, the stain on the ceiling that seemed to be taking on the shape of a one-legged man as she looked up at it, the eye-wiping toupeed ancient, a car revving up out in the street, the dampness of her own body. Everything connected with seeing, hearing, touching, contributed to her joy. When he levered himself off her and words came, they were inevitably clichés, because no words could express the experience.

"Okay?" He stood naked beside the bed, wiping himself.

"Just wonderful." Later she said, "No words for what I feel, none at all, you know that." She stroked his shoulder. "Look at me, I want to ask you something. We're good together, aren't we, it isn't just me?"

"Told you, fantastic."

"Better than with other people? It's all right, I know there must be other people."

"The tops."

"I'm not very experienced, you must know that."

His fingers traced the outline of her nose, lips, chin. "Could be all the time. You don't want it."

She was about to say indignantly that of course she did, then understood what he meant. "That man, Willem, he asked too much money. Much too much."

"Yeah, I spoke to him on the blower, he told me. About the dosh. Tell me something, you got it wrong."

"*I* got it wrong?"

"Saying no like that. He just, you know, he was just asking, cutting a deal."

"I couldn't bargain." She thought how strange it was that she could contemplate Victor's death, but was horrified by the idea of haggling about the price.

"Yeah, I know. Like with the room here, you wouldn't think of it." He patted her hand, laughed. "I go for that. So I done it for you. Did it."

"What?"

"Bargained. Like I did at this crummy joint. He'll do it for six. Three and three. I got him down to that." She said nothing. "Look, what I hear, all I hear, this geezer's special. He's got a reputation, not all mouth, does what he says. And he's not just muscle either, you wanted a way to keep you out of it, he says he's put propositions that'll do that, only you wouldn't listen. Then when it's done he'll be away, no need for you to know where, you never met him, nothing to do with him. What do you think?" She did not reply, for she was not capable of thinking anything. The enormity of what was suggested, what she was requesting and considering, overwhelmed her. "The second half, could be he'd arrange for it to be paid in some bank abroad, depends where he is."

She said, "It would take almost all the money I have, we

shouldn't be able to go to California." When she told him just how much she had in her current and deposit accounts he looked astonished, then crestfallen. She had to explain to him that it would be a little while before the Old Man's money came to Victor. He sat on the bed and listened to what she had to say with the sulky disappointment of a child.

"That's it then, innit?" She touched his shoulder uncertainly, said she loved him, was rewarded with a brief smile. He brightened when she said it was possible that she might be able to borrow on the strength of a coming inheritance. "You mean, s'posing we was in some place, California say, in what, six months, you'd have the dosh?" Something like that, she said, but any investigation would show that they were living together, and if there were any suspicions she would be an obvious suspect and so would he. He said, still sullenly, that he supposed she was right.

"Your idea, wannit, now you're saying forget it, right?"

She hated to see him looking miserable, but she remembered Foster, and other things she'd read about where the plans had gone wrong. "Unless there's a way by which everyone thinks it was an accident."

"Willem told me he put up some ideas."

"He did. Perhaps one of them would work, I don't know. But it would have to be foolproof, no suspicion. If the police found out I'd taken all the money from my account and asked why, what would I say?"

"Yeah, yeah, I see that. But seems to me you don't want it anyway, you're thinking how would it be in California or some place, you and me all the time, having to teach me, going places you'd have to explain stuff to me, me doing things wrong, you wouldn't want that, wouldn't want me around all the time . . ."

He went on about his ignorance, and saying he knew she didn't believe he'd ever do anything, but he'd show her if he only had a bit of money to start, until she couldn't bear it and said, stop, stop, that wasn't the way it was at all, he'd got it hopelessly wrong, she wanted nothing more than to be with him all the time, it was just thinking of how to manage it. She heard herself pleading with him not to be angry. He shook his head.

"See, when you first said it I thought, no way, won't work and I don't want any part in it. Then, you see the way it is at home, Mum's all right I s'pose, but there's days she makes me that mad I could clock her one, and when I met you, well, it was sort of, I knew it was what I wanted. So when there's a chance it could come off, if you want it like I do"—She said again that she did. "I reckon people got a right to be happy, if they can make it together it should be okay by everyone."

The childishness of it alarmed and delighted her, and made her as reluctant as he was to name the thing they weren't mentioning, the death it all depended on. When he ended by saying it was no good, she heard herself telling him that perhaps she would talk to Willem again, see if he would—she didn't know how to put it, and said *reconsider his terms*. But Billy shook his head.

"You don't get it, do you? No use talking like that, I said he's a pro."

"But you told me he was asking too much, expecting to make a deal."

"Yeah, but well, see, I cut him down by half, and that was only because he'd do a quick job and then out. See, once he's out, gone to Brazil or Argentina or one of those places, can't remember all the names, he's safe there and so are you. He told me he can't line a job up he'll be gone next week." She heard herself asking, almost pleading, that Billy should talk to him again, tell him the position, saying if he would only wait a few weeks—

"No use saying that, he'd put the phone down. Three and three, that's the bottom line, you want to talk to him again?" With that feeling of unreality overwhelmingly strong she said yes, but only if he could convince her he had a foolproof plan, one that left her free of suspicion. She was rewarded with his smile, an embrace so tight it made her breathless, then a drop into caution.

"Mind, I dunno he'll take it on, he may call it off, or maybe I can't get hold of him, he's gone. S'pose it's okay though, should I say same time tomorrow, same place?" She said yes.

They were silent on the drive back, until she dropped him off just before they got to the Estate. Then he said, "Same as before. I get hold of him I give you a bell, whoever answers you or him I say 'Sorry, wrong number' if it's okay. If I can't make contact or he says no I say 'I want to speak to Harry' and you say no Harry here. Get it? Okay then. Remember, you belong to me." He put two fingers on her cheek, was out of the car and round the corner in a moment.

Back at home, although she realized now that she had never really thought of Green Diamonds as home, and it sometimes seemed to her that she had had no home since she left Three Gables, the feeling of unreality persisted. She looked into the bedroom glass, and thought: can this really be the face of a woman planning murder, or am I still playing a game like the one with the letters from Philo? If she looked into the glass long enough perhaps another woman would appear, one impatient of game-playing who would show her exactly what she had to do. She said to the face in the glass, "I know you're there, no point in hiding, tell me what you think I should do." But the face gave no help, did not change expression, so that she could not be sure what it wanted her to do. Did it want the game she was playing with Billy and Willem to become real? Or should she make an excuse and back away? I don't know, she told the face in the glass, truly I don't know. Then she added with emphasis: and *you're* no help. At that the face smiled, and she supposed she was smiling too.

She drank a strong gin to steady her nerves, but when the telephone rang it was several seconds before she could lift the instrument. It was Victor, saying he was going to a meeting with Johnny and Clive, they'd get something to eat, he might be late. He asked if she was all right. Yes, she said, why shouldn't she be?

"You sound a bit odd, that's all."

"Off beam?"

"If you like. No word from your favourite policeman?"

"Of course not, why should there be? And he's not a favourite of mine."

"My mistake. Look after yourself. I should be back soon after nine."

When she put down the telephone she thought again about the photographs, and a shudder ran through her. The other who had refused to offer any opinion in the looking glass, said she knew what she had to do if she didn't want to go on living with Victor.

The evening stretched ahead, a long void to be filled. Somehow she got through it, read a couple of chapters in a book, watched TV and ate an omelette, watched more TV. The call came at ten o'clock, Victor not back, when she had decided to go to bed. She had drunk two more gins, and this time her hand was steady. Billy's voice said "Hello," she replied with the same word, he said "Sorry, wrong number," and rang off.

She felt perfectly calm. This is almost real, she thought, but not quite. I'm near the edge, not over it. Tomorrow I can still make it a game.

Again she was in bed when Victor returned, just after eleven o'clock. He opened the bedroom door and called her name, but she made no answer. When the door closed she distinctly saw a merry-go-round, horses, camels and elephants going up and down, round and round and up and down while a man whose face was invisible cranked an engine and the music asked, "*Is* it a game, I can *make* it a game, *is* it a game or not?" She put on the light, got out of bed, swallowed two of the tablets that had been prescribed when she had her nervous breakdown, to be taken at times of stress, and fell asleep.

AFTERWARDS

"Don't you read the papers?"

Ron Hinks was short, bald and had a squint. He squinted now at Craxton, then shook his head.

"Listen to the news on radio?"

"All talk, nobody saying anything, never listen. What I do mostly, mind my own business. But I'm here now, ain't I?" He looked around Craxton's bare office, and at the hard-faced man behind the desk.

"You employed Gay as a driver?"

"C'n I smoke?" It was not really a question. He lighted up, squinted at Craxton with one eye, the other straying to a photograph of police cadets on the wall to the detective's left. "One of two, two I employed, call it that. I gotta partner, see, name of Joe Winters. Got ideas, Joe has, I do the work, he takes the money." This was a joke. He laughed. Craxton did not smile. "Always the way that, so I've found, maybe been unlucky. Mind, Joe's clever, give him that. He thinks up this refresher course, brush up your Highway Code and that. Who wants it, I said, but turns out he's right, so this Billy Gay's

155

one of the drivers. Joe knew about him, says he can drive, but got a record so you wanta watch him. So can he drive? Maybe he can, but he's full of talk, all piss and wind, how he's gonna make a lot of dough, that kind of stuff. So what happens? He smashes up one of my motors, talking when he shoulda been using the dual, so I says out."

"Mrs. Lassiter was one of the clients he drove. What did he say about her?"

"Said she fancied him. I told him to keep his hands to himself. Don't know any more, mind me own business."

"Did he say anything else about money?"

"Only when I told him he was finished, out, go away and don't come back. Said he'd been leaving anyway, got a big deal on, going abroad, no more pissing about for a few quid."

"Did he give any details? Say he was going with anybody or how he was getting the money?"

"Talked about going to America. Didn't pay attention. Can't remember names."

"California?"

"Could be, I dunno. Nothing to me, I ain't going there."

"Did he say 'I' or 'we,' I'm going or we're going?"

Ron Hinks's eyes squinted horribly all around the office. "Could be he said 'we,' but I dunno."

"You don't know much, do you?"

"Mister, I make a living, I run a garage, I got a partner makes the money out of it. I know about motors, never fiddled one in my life, you won't find nobody bought a motor from Ron Hinks wasn't a genuine goer. That's my business, and I mind my business. This stuff you're asking about, I don't take any interest. What this boy says or where he was going or what happened to him, I didn't give a fart then and I don't now."

PART FOUR

The Other

1

Morning. She got out of bed, went through the mechanisms of the early hours, then dressing gown, slippers, table laid, bread in toaster and croissants in oven. She was aware that the day was unusually dark and that an unlocatable buzzing was going on somewhere or other. Buzz buzz—of course, the oven was making the noise to tell her the croissants were ready, but did the oven buzz to give such information, or was the sound in her head? She had filled the kettle too full and instead of cutting out as it should have done it spilled over. Things were going wrong. And where was Victor? But here he came, neat as ever, wearing a perfectly awful bow tie. Breakfast ready? he asked, and in the next breath, Like my tie, know who gave it to me? The buzzing went on even though she had taken out the croissants and it distracted her, she turned her head away from Victor's face which had suddenly become very large as he whispered into her ear: "Billy gave it to me, would you believe it, you're not the only one he likes, isn't he just fantastic, fantastic, fantastic . . ."

She woke crying out, "You're not the only one," looked

159

desperately at the flower patterns on wallpaper, curtains, dressing table frill, and thought of Dahlia and Larkspur, Magnolia, Rose and Hyacinth. Her head was splitting in half with a pain that ran down it at dead center. Her hands shook. When she stood up the room at once began to shiver in sympathy with her hands. She got to the wash-basin, splashed water over her face and arms, felt a little better. She heard voices, or perhaps they were only in her head. She opened her bedroom door. A man was in Victor's room going through his wardrobe, feeling in the pockets of suits. The man looked around and nodded as she went in, holding the door to steady herself. When she asked him who he was he said, "Maitland, Fraud Squad."

"You're going through my husband's clothes." He nodded agreement at this statement of the obvious, opened a chest of drawers full of shirts. "What are you doing, *why* are you here?"

"Better ask Sergeant Higgs. Out there talking to your husband now."

She went back to her bedroom, put on a jumper and skirt. Coffee, she thought as she made an uncertain way to the living room, coffee is the only thing. But perhaps this was a second dream which would blend with the first, she would find Victor eating a croissant at the table, Billy would be sharing his breakfast. Those were the voices she heard, perhaps they would be embracing. A flash of lightning dazzled her, she put a hand over her eyes. The pain in her head was excruciating.

"There you are." She removed her head. The light, a little less painful now that she knew its origin, came from the twin track lamps. Victor was at the table eating a croissant and a man sat opposite drinking coffee, but the man was not Billy, of course not. He was somebody she had never seen, a barrel-chested man with a round red face. Victor got up, came over, put an arm around her shoulder. "I tried to wake you but couldn't, you just turned over and murmured something. Do you feel all right? Frankly, you look terrible."

She croaked, splitting head, sleeping pills, overdose, coffee. Then she was at the table gulping black liquid. She said to the red-faced man, "I don't understand. Why are you here?"

The man opened his mouth, but it was Victor who replied. "This is Sergeant Higgs. He has a search warrant, and he wants me to—what's the phrase, Sergeant?"

"Come down to the station for a chat." The Sergeant's voice was surprisingly quiet, almost delicate.

She said, "A chat? What about?"

"Just my question." Victor ate the last mouthful of the croissant. "The Sergeant doesn't know, or so he says, but he was kind enough to agree I could have breakfast first and, as you can see, joined me for a cup of coffee. My chief worry, as I told him, was that you simply refused to wake up. How many of those pills did you take?"

"Two. Stupid of me, doctor said only one. Victor, what are they looking for?"

"In the old phrase, you could search me, I've no idea. I'm not sure the Sergeant has either." He looked questioningly at Sergeant Higgs, who stared blankly back. "Perhaps you should ask your friend Craxton. He's the man in charge, is that right, Sergeant?"

"Don't know why you should think that, sir. We're Fraud Squad, nothing to do with Mr. Craxton. Time to go." He said apologetically to Judith, "I'm afraid we'll need to look at your room, Mrs. Lassiter." The man who had been in Victor's bedroom returned, and called the Sergeant outside. Judith finished her coffee. Her head seemed still split in two, one side ached much more than the other. Victor leaned across the table. "I don't believe that about Craxton. Ask him to call his dogs off. Say they'll find nothing, because there's nothing to find."

Before she could reply the Sergeant returned, and asked if Victor had a license for the revolver in his bedroom.

"It belonged to my father and yes, I have a license. Don't

161

ask me where it is because I don't know, but I do have a license and if you want me to produce it—"

"Not sure that'll be necessary, sir." There suddenly appeared in his hand, with a conjurer's legerdemain, an envelope Judith recognized. "Would these be your property, Mr. Lassiter?"

For a moment, only a moment, Victor flinched as if punched in the stomach. "They are, yes, and they're nothing to do with you."

"I think I must take charge of them, sir. You'll be given a receipt, and if it's as you say, of course they'll be returned."

Victor's voice was calm, but his face was very white. He said to Judith, "Ring Nick Williams, tell him the police have a search warrant, won't say what they're looking for or why they're doing it, and ask him to meet me at the station." He turned to Sergeant Higgs. "I want it on record that I protest against the dictatorial nature of this whole proceeding, and that I shall take it up with your superior officer."

"Noted by me, and I'm sure by your lady wife as well. Now, Mr. Lassiter, let's get moving."

Victor took a couple of steps towards her, seemed to think better of it, and was gone. Sergeant Higgs, with a little bob of the head, went too. The man who had been in Victor's room reappeared, and at the same moment another man came in from the front hall. One was dark, the other fair, but they wore the same dark shiny suits and had the same air of carnivores who have scented blood. The man from Victor's room— and her room—said, "Any joy?" and the other made a gesture that might have meant anything. She asked what they were looking for. The man who had spoken said, "Shan't know till we find it," then "Sorry about the intrusion, has to be done." She saw the other man had a large blue cardboard folder, asked what he had in it, and he said just a few papers that might be interesting and that she'd get a receipt for everything they took. *Receipt* seemed to be a magic word, everything was all right it seemed if they provided a receipt. She imagined them taking away the bed and saying no need to worry, she'd be given a receipt.

"What about the roof space?" That was the first man. Pain thudded in her head. "Need a chair, do we?" She told him there was a small ladder that pulled down. They nodded, left her, and she tried to remember what it was she should be doing. Nick Williams, their solicitor.

Nick Williams's voice on the telephone said "Yes," then stopped her as she began an explanation. "I know about it. Best not to talk on the telephone, but I can tell you at least two other people are being questioned, maybe more. Remember, at this point it's only questioning. What about? I'd very much like to know, I'm pressing the authorities to say just why they're giving my clients this hassle. Offices are being searched as well, of course. But not to worry, if my guess is right, Victor will have made his statement and be home again by—oh, say by lunchtime. No more now. I'll be in touch."

If she closed her eyes and opened them again, it occurred to her, all this would go away. The idea that it was a dream, like the buzzing and the kettle that spilled over, persisted. She did keep her eyes shut tight for what seemed like minutes and was aware only of the pain in her head, almost all on one side now and certainly much reduced, but still a pain like—what?—like hammers beating a gentle tattoo, and then suddenly the tattoo no longer gentle, shaking her whole body as she tried to accommodate it and willed the hammers to soften. And they did soften. She heard a cough, opened her eyes. Intruder number one, Maitland, Fraud Squad, stood in front of her brushing dust off his suit with his hand. There was no refuge in the dream. Maitland said he and his colleague were sorry to have bothered her, finished now. Then they were gone, really gone. She closed her eyes again, heard the telephone ringing.

It was Debbie, Debbie at her most theatrical, and so confused in speech that Judith could not at first understand what she was saying. She felt herself to be a model of calmness as she replied to Debbie's questions.

"Yes, Victor's gone to the station to answer some questions, and Nick Williams—yes, I've spoken to him—knew about it and said he thought he'd be out by lunchtime. I don't really know any more than that, and Nick Williams said we shouldn't speak too freely, don't know who's listening. Nick said at least two other people—"

At that point Debbie stopped her, shrieking that of course one was Johnny, hadn't they come and almost bashed their door in, and the other was Clive. But did Judith know how much *they* knew, had her friend Craxton told her—

At which point *she* stopped Debbie, said they shouldn't be talking like this, Nick Williams had advised against it as she'd just said.

"Oh, bugger Nick Williams. Didn't he tell you *anything*, that bloody policeman of yours?"

"I don't think he's concerned with it personally, Debbie, he was just trying to warn me. Perhaps it's the trouble with Nethersole, that's all I can think of."

"Nethersole," Debbie positively shrieked. "Why do you keep talking about him, it's stuff that's been going on for years." And at that point she stopped suddenly, was silent as if she realized the stupidity of talking like this on the telephone. When she spoke again it was in a different tone, tremulous and tear-laden.

"I'm not religious, you know that, but I've been praying, on my knees hoping that everything comes all right for Johnny." A sob, or what sounded like one, came over the line. "I love him, you see. Doesn't matter what he's done or what I've done, I love him, I shall never love anyone else. He's a good man and you've got a good man too, you get down on your knees, Judith Lassiter, and pray he comes back and there's no trouble."

If there is one thing I shall not be doing, Judith thought

when she put down the receiver, it is praying for Victor. She looked up the number of Wyfleet police headquarters, dialed, asked to speak to Craxton, was told he was busy, left her name and asked him to ring back.

What else to do? If Victor and the Mad Hatter and other people had been involved in some kind of swindle and went to prison, would it help her? She could not see that it would. Life with Billy in California would be no nearer, for Victor would still control his money. Unable to sit down, she walked about the house, putting things straight in her bedroom and Victor's. The once-locked drawer was open, the Mauser reposing on what seemed the same papers she had looked at, only the envelope with the photographs was gone. In her room, all the clothes in the wardrobe had been examined and put back, not in the right order, boxes of powder had been emptied. She wondered whether this was just customary procedure or if they had been looking for gold or jewels bought by Victor with money illegally obtained. The idea of Victor buying her a ten thousand pound necklace and then burying it in a box of powder made her giggle. Giggling made her head throb. Then she felt indignant. What right had these pigs to stick their snouts into her wardrobe, nose about among her clothes, dip their dirty trotters into boxes of powder? The image once summoned up she saw Maitland Fraud Squad clearly as a pig on all fours, little nostrils sniffing her womanly scent, giving excited squeals as he dipped into her powder. She thought if she closed her eyes pig Maitland would go away, but instead he was joined by the companion pig wearing a dark shiny suit very tight on his pig body. This pig waved a blue folder and began to open it. She was not dreaming but *seeing* all this, and only with much effort forced her eyes open, crying out words she was able to hear: "Stop it, stop it." I am two people, she thought, one of them seeing, hearing, watching, and the other. . . What did the other do? Nothing! The other was the other, the image that refused to become visible in the looking glass.

165

Eyelids were wrenched up like shutters. She was in the bedroom. The telephone was ringing. Time elapsed, seconds or minutes she could not tell, as she watched her hand crawling towards the telephone, lifting it.

Craxton's voice said, "Mrs. Lassiter. Craxton. How can I help you?"

She said something about Victor, and the reply was the phrase about helping with enquiries. "Is he under arrest?" She heard herself asking this, the other heard her and was impressed by her coolness.

"I said, helping with enquiries." In a different tone he said, "Are you all right?"

"Probably, yes. Not quite myself." He made no comment. "Is it possible—I wondered—"

"Yes?"

"To see you."

The silence seemed so long (but the other, watching and observing, was aware her judgement of time was not what it should be) that she thought he must have gone. Then he spoke rapidly and said half an hour, Goat and Compasses, off the High Street, know it? She must have said yes although she was not aware of it, nor could she remember ever seeing the pub. She wondered if their conversation had really taken place, or was simply all in her head. But she was able, or the other was able, to drive the car efficiently, and to find the little pub without difficulty. She was sitting in a dark corner with a half pint of bitter in front of her, something that again was odd because as the other should have known, she never drank bitter.

She had been there a minute, or perhaps fifteen minutes, when he came in, saw her, got a pint of beer at the bar and joined her.

"This has to be quick," he said. "By rights I shouldn't be here. Just that you sounded odd on the phone, as if you were in shock."

"I don't think I'm in shock. Oh no, not at all." She drank some of the bitter, was surprised to find it had no taste, said cheers.

"It shouldn't come as a shock. I warned you."

She felt herself smiling. Was it possible that she could also *see* herself smiling? She knew that if she closed her eyes that would happen. "I'm quite calm," she said. "You can see I'm quite calm." She sipped the bitter again. "This is very nice."

"So why did you want to see me?"

"I just wanted." She tried to think of a reason, a reasonable reason. "Because you like me. And I like you."

"I wish I could believe it."

"Victor's in a lot of trouble, isn't he? Going to prison?"

"It's not my pigeon, I'm not in the Fraud Squad. None of it's my business." He drank beer, almost banged his glass on the table. "I'd like to go to bed with you, you must know that's why I'm here when I shouldn't be, and from what I've seen you don't have much luck going to bed with your husband." He waited for a response but got none. "There are limits though. Your friends are in a lot of trouble, I'll tell you that, but which of 'em will go down or if any of 'em will is guesswork. That any use to you? I just don't know what you're after."

"Neither do I."

"Oh for Christ's sake, make some sense."

"You see, I'm off beam."

"What?"

"You said I was off beam." She heard the words come out roguishly, flirtatiously. "Going to bed, it's not the kind of thing I do." Liar, the other said. "But I might consider it." Oh liar, liar, you'd never betray Billy.

He stood up. "That's it. You're wasting my time, I shouldn't be surprised if you wasted your husband's time too. And I don't like cock teasers."

Then he was gone, his glass still half full. She finished what was in her own glass, then drank his. In the course of doing so she suddenly saw what must happen, how the police investigation of Victor and the others provided a solution, a perfect solution, to her problem. She was so pleased with the discovery that she ordered and drank another half pint of beer, that mercifully tasteless beer. Then she drove to Hastings.

2

Willem today might have been a different person, or perhaps it was that the other saw him, and looked with different eyes. He seemed distinctly smarter and less grubby, wearing a grey suit and blue shirt with matching tie. He had also shaved, something made obvious by two or three bits of dried blood round the jaw. Before, he had looked like a badly paid schoolmaster having a day out, today he had the appearance of a man wearing his best suit when applying for a job. Yet, as the other detachedly remarked, he did not seem nervous, briskly businesslike rather. And the shark's smile, when it came, transformed him instantly into a predator.

The same adenoidal girl waited on them. He stopped her recital of the menu when she came to welsh rarebit. "That's for me. And put a poached egg on top of it." He said to Judith, "A toasted teacake for you." When the girl had gone he said, "Looks bad, just one of us eating."

"I don't want it."

"See when it comes. If you don't eat it, I shall. But you just

169

make a little effort, eh?" She began to say there was something she should tell him, but he stopped her. "No, something *I* tell *you*. I stay here only another two, maybe three days. Somebody, call him a client, in West Germany has a little job for me. West Germany, wrong, you don't say it, it's all Germany now, but this client lives in the West and has a claim on a property in the East. Seems his family owned a house and land near Dresden fifty years ago, and now they'd like it back. People in the house, East Germans I still call them, say no." She asked if it wasn't a matter for lawyers, and got the shark smile. "They take months, maybe years. I shall try to persuade—" he lingered over the word, giving it three syllables, *per-su-ade*—"the tenant to move out."

"It's only a tenant?"

"He's been in occupation some years, but my client thinks he is a tenant. So do I."

She was startled when he closed one eye in a wink. His eyes—why had she not noticed them before?—had the wide watchful look of a toad's, their gaze neither hostile nor friendly but unblinking. "*So*," he said, and the emphasis made him sound very unEnglish. "*So* I come here today because our friend says you might think again. But if we do business, you think fast. In three days I am gone."

The girl brought the food, she poured tea, he attacked the welsh rarebit with controlled ferocity, shook his head. "This egg, cooked too much, hard. Never mind. Well?"

At the back of her head, or to one side of it, the engines of pain still throbbed gently. It was a job to formulate words and phrases, but she managed it, speaking slowly.

"Things have changed, that's what I wanted to tell you. Last time—" She paused, not wanting to say that she had distrusted him. "—last time I was worried about all your—" She hesitated again, then found the word—"suggestions. You understand, there must be no possibility of my involvement."

"You said." He finished a piece of welsh rarebit. "Hit and run."

"Suppose you were seen."

"I should not be seen. And it would not be my car." The shark smile came and went.

"I don't know. Anyway I have thought of something else, something better. Today the police took my husband away for questioning, searched the house. There are other people involved, I think they will bring charges." She drank some tea. It had no more taste than the beer. "My husband, Victor, might run away. Go abroad to escape prison. You see?" He nodded, eyes unblinking. "You used to be a sailor, I thought you would have a friend and could arrange to hire a boat. Then there is no sign of Victor, he never reappears." Calm deserted her, she felt the excitement in her raised voice, put a hand over her mouth to check herself. "He'd have a reason for disappearing, don't you see? And soon the police would give up looking, they'd suppose he'd had plastic surgery or something, just leave the file open or whatever they call it, in case he turned up some time. What's the matter?" She could not interpret his gesture.

"You don't want it?"

"What? Oh have it." She could have screamed, but the other said calm, stay calm. She pushed the teacake towards him. He cut it in half, spoke.

"Very clever. But won't do." She had to wait while he ate part of the teacake, wiped his mouth. Then he said, "No money."

"What do you mean?"

"Our subject disappears, has good reasons, the police accept he goes out of the country, pass it on to Interpol, they don't find him, the case lies on the file. Very good." Again she had to wait while he ate another piece of teacake. "Very good but no good. If there is no body you wait a long time, seven years perhaps, anyway a long time, before you are able to claim, I'm not sure of the word, the estate? You are English, you should know."

Of course she did know, how could she have been so stupid?

As she looked across the table at the respectable ordinary man in a grey suit who was now gulping down his second cup of tea, she felt a mixture of hatred and respect. And suddenly she believed that he was what he said, somebody who injured, maimed and killed people for money, as a job. Why had she ever disbelieved when she read every week of murder squads who went around killing stray children on the streets of Brazil and Guatemala, commissioned to do so by businessmen worried that the children were keeping customers from their shops? Now he was talking again.

"*So* you see it won't do the way you have it, but it is still very good, very clever. Only there must be a body, you understand. Here is how we do it. I have a friend with a boat, you are right, more than one friend, better you don't know too much about them. This is the way it goes. I give a telephone call to the subject, tell him I have information of interest to him about—you must tell me a name, something that could help him—"

"I suppose if there was police corruption, he could use that. You could mention a policeman named Craxton, he's an Inspector or Chief Inspector or something, but—"

"Be quiet. I say I know something interesting about this Craxton, but I have to meet him, perhaps I ask for a little money. We arrange a place. I know one or two." Again the shark's smile. "Better you don't know the rest."

"But I *want* to know."

"All right, but perhaps you won't like. We meet, he gets in my car."

"How do you—"

"I have a Colt thirty-eight. Then handcuffs, a little ether, he has a little boat ride, drowns, his body washes up two, three days later. A place off the coast where the sea brings everything ashore." The shark's smile again. "He will be wearing a wet suit. On the shore will be his clothes. In them is a typed message saying a boat will pick him up eleven o'clock at night fifty yards off shore." He stopped suddenly. "He can swim?"

"Yes, he's a good swimmer."

"Little things like that, they mustn't be forgotten. So what happened? He means to disappear, arranges it, something goes wrong, he drowns."

"Why does he leave the note?"

Willem shrugged. "He is careless."

"The police will suspect something."

"Why should they? He made plans to escape, they went wrong, he drowned. There will be water in the lungs, a natural death." He pushed away the teacup. "I like it, yes, very much. And you, what do you think?"

Off beam, she thought, you're off beam. The other, who had been observing her all the time and who had disapproved, she felt, of all her questions, took over now and said quite calmly, "It keeps me out of it."

"You like it? Good. You have brought a photograph of the subject? Other details also, an address, something about his habits, his routine." Yes, she had jotted down details of Victor's routine as he called it and put them in an envelope along with two snaps and their address. The envelope had been in her bag when she had talked with Craxton, something she knew the other had relished. Now she took it out and gave it to Willem. He gave his nod and said, "So?"

Now came the part she had prepared in the car, although it was the other and not she who thought the words would ever be spoken. "Our friend told you the most I could pay."

"Three and three, yes."

The other admired her coolness—or was it she who admired the other's coolness? "I will draw the first installment from the bank tomorrow. For the second, you must tell me where it should be paid."

"It will be the Hamburg Credit Trust, the name Edgar Dunant." He forestalled her question. "I have accounts in several names. This one is Edgar Dunant. Remember it, do not write it down."

Now the crux. "I pay the first installment to our friend. He will pass it to you when he is sure the plan is going to work."

"You don't trust me?"

She might have cried out, "Of course I don't," but the other said coolly, "There's no need for trust on either side. I do trust our friend. I hope you do too. When he is sure you have done the first part of what you say, he pays you the money. All right?" He made an irritated gesture, said nothing. "He will have the money tomorrow. When he is satisfied he gives it to you."

The shark's smile once more. "You drive a good bargain. Very well."

Five minutes later they parted. This time she paid for the tea.

3

The dreamlike quality of my experience—she spoke these words aloud as she drove back at leisure from Hastings, feeling replete, satisfied, as after making love with Billy. This dreamlike quality she found everywhere, in fields and trees that seemed misty, richly yet softly coloured in their vagueness. The asphalt of the road glowed as if illuminated from within, the Fiesta's engine sound was delicate instead of harsh, even the lorries that passed her seemed more like children's toys enlarged than the thunderous beasts she knew them to be. She tried to remember lines she had once read about the world new-made, but could get no further than those few words, and repeated them over and over while the Fiesta purred approval. She did not contemplate the future that would be spent in California or Calcutta or Cairo, or anywhere outside this country where an essential part of herself had been buried underground for so long. In another country, under a hot sun, she would flower.

Nor did she contemplate the present, which was all decided now, except to feel that she must be very nice to Victor be-

cause there was so little time left for him. And although she
thought about Billy, she felt she was no longer dependent on
him, perhaps never had been so. Billy had been the means to
an end, as the other was aware. In the sunlight of his love she
had flowered, but for how much longer would she need that
sunlight? You said going to bed is not the kind of thing you
do, the other reminded her, but really it is. There was no
reason why Billy should fail her, but if that happened she
liked the assurance given by the other that there was no need
to worry. I am off beam, most tremendously off beam, she
said to the other, and I'm pleased that is so.

When she got home Victor was there. He had been grilled,
as he termed it, for nearly four hours, and looked unusually
pale. He was constantly on the telephone to Clive, Johnny
and other people whose first names meant nothing to her. She
was conscious of the approval of the other as she made herself
tremendously nice to him, pouring drinks, asking what he
would like for supper, briefly stroking his hair so that he
looked at her in surprise. He abandoned the telephone, spoke
to her.

"It's all nonsense, you know, they've got nothing, a storm
in a teacup." She did not comment on that, but said he should
be careful about what was said on the telephone, it might be
tapped.

"You think so? Still, you heard me, I said nothing out of
line, nor did Johnny or Dick or anyone. Did your friend
Craxton say the line was tapped?"

I'd like to go to bed with you, you know that—she savoured
the phrase, thought of telling Victor but the other said no. So
she said of course not, and asked who Dick was.

"Dick Casement, who else?"

"That little dummy I talked to at the Rotary dinner, you
mean he's mixed up in this?"

"He's—" He began again. "Nobody's *mixed up* in anything,
none of us has done anything wrong. A lot of fuss about some

176

contracts, that's all. You're taking a lot of interest, you sure none of this is going back to that copper?"

She put her hand on her heart. "I solemnly swear that not a word of our conversation will be communicated to a living soul. Or a dead one."

"I believe you. Friends again?"

When she said yes, she saw the easy charmer whose smiling good nature had attracted her years ago. "When I said I loved you, I meant every word. There are different sorts of love, that's all. I wish you could recognize that."

Oh, I do recognize it, either she or the other thought but did not say, indeed I do. When he said there seemed something different about her, so that she seemed distant yet strangely at the same time more accessible, more friendly, she was conscious for the first time of her superiority to him (or was it the other who was superior?), and of the coarse simplicity with which he exercised his professional skill as a charmer. It is not that I see through you, she thought, more that the impact made by your personality on mine, which once seemed so great, is now barely visible. She meditated on this while making a sauce for a dish of veal medallions, followed by fruit salad enlivened by a dash of kirsch.

Victor said this deserved something better than the plonk he had put out, but that if he took a claret from the cold room now it would barely have the chill off. Would she consider a white burgundy, a Meursault that should be a match for the sauce with the veal? She went along with the fiction that she knew something about wine and said yes. Victor said the veal was perfectly cooked. They ate in harmony.

He was pouring Remy-Martin for them both when she remembered that she had made no arrangement to let Billy know what had happened that afternoon, and at almost the moment of this recollection the telephone rang. He answered it, said "Not at all," then to her: "Wrong number." Man or woman, she said, and he answered man. When she wanted to know the exact words he paused before saying "I can't remember," then "Do you know who it was?"

"Of course not."

"He said 'Sorry, wrong number,' something like that. Was it Craxton?" She told him not to be silly, he had Craxton on the brain, she had asked only out of curiosity. She could not resist adding: "I don't ask if Dick was one of the people in those photographs. I mean, not in the ones I saw, but if he was one of your group, in other pictures."

At that he visibly flinched. "I said they're nothing to do with my life here, I wouldn't be stupid enough to compromise myself like that." He paused, then said, "About the photographs."

With those words spoken she saw them all again vividly, leafed through them in her mind, and all the pleasure of the evening (and yes, it had been enjoyable, an echo of the good days with Victor long ago) was replaced by those awful images of Victor the slave, Victor with penis in mouth, the Victor she did not want to know or think about. What was he saying?

"They're not important, you know, just a physical need. Otherwise they mean nothing, I'm not involved, try to believe that."

She said she would try. They drank the brandy and then, with characteristic mock gallantry he kissed her hand, and said how much he had enjoyed the evening. She said truly that she had enjoyed it too. It did not seem at all strange that she should say such a thing when she had that day hired a hit man to kill him.

4

After that she moved on a course as inevitable as that of a plane on automatic pilot or a bomb directed by laser beam. Yet alongside this course with the end result she avoided naming even to herself, her usual life went its way. Friendly relations with Victor were maintained at breakfast. Eating his croissants, he said they were a couple, knew each other's ways, it would be absurd for them to lead separate lives. Whimsically, smiling, he used the croissants as proof of this. Who else would know exactly how long he liked a croissant to stay in the oven, or would ring the changes on jam and honey, with an occasional diversion into marmalade and quince cheese? Before leaving he kissed her more tenderly than usual.

"Last night settled something for me," he said. "I felt we were in harmony, and that you thought so too." With no feeling of betrayal she said that was right, and when he told her there was no need to worry about the other affair responded truthfully that she was not worried. Then she watched the Lagonda go down the drive, as usual a little too fast.

After that there was Patty, Patty with Derek who this morning had a black eye and a bandaged leg. He hardly spoke before settling in front of TV cartoons, two biscuits and a glass of lemonade by his side. Patty unburdened herself over coffee.

"It's Carl see, when he gets his rag out, like if anything goes wrong, he don't mind what he does. Told you he used to be in this group Fighting Foreigners, di'nt I? They used to get in a lotta trouble, kind of looked for it, know what I mean? Well, Rocky's been away so Carl's been staying, and I dunno I s'pose something's gone wrong, when it does he has to take it out on somebody, I mean you get people like that, can't help it. I keep a knife handy when I see he's in a mood and I tell him you touch me, and you know what you'll get. Broke a couple of my ribs once knocking me about and I said never again, so I got this knife and if he tried anything I'd use it, and he knows I mean it.

"Only last night, see, Angie, lives almost opposite, she says come over look at a new catalogue she's got, mail order, all sorts of stuff you buy it straight from the factory, dresses they say they're fashion models and that. So we have a drink, Angie and me, and I'm away oh say couple of hours, and Carl turns up. He's been staying away and I'm not expecting him am I, or I'd been there. But I'm not and he wants something to eat, nothing he fancies in the fridge, and he says Derek was cheeky and I dunno perhaps he was, Derek don't like him. So he starts beating up on Derek, and I dunno what woulda happened I'd not come home, reckon Carl'd have smashed him up good and proper." Judith asked what had happened to Derek's leg. "Derek he gives Carl a bit of a punch, so he just throws the kid across the room and he hits his leg on the corner of a sorta coffee table, got it through another catalogue called Bargain Basement, you seen that one, the other one was Cost Cutters, they reckon they undercut the big stores fifty percent. Anyway we got this coffee table, sorta marble only it isn't, know what I mean? And Derek catches his leg on the corner, lot of blood, you know what Carl said? 'Let the little sod bleed to death.'

180

Course he wouldn't a done but maybe I ought to go to the RSPCA or what they call it, what do you think?"

"It's the NSPCC, children not animals."

"Oh yeah." Patty dunked a biscuit in her coffee, ate it. Her face was happy, unlined.

Judith felt a sympathy that was distant, uninvolved. She said it wasn't easy to see just what the NSPCC could do.

"Okay I have another biscuit? Ta, thanks. I dunno, you go to these places, they make a lot of fuss, get nosy, ask all sorts of stuff. I reckon I'll leave it for now. He's not always like that, you know, Carl, doesn't like seeing Derek around."

"Perhaps it makes him feel responsible."

Patty snorted. "Some chance. But we have some good times. Rocky too, Rocky's nice, you'd like Rocky." She dunked the other biscuit, ate it, finished the coffee. "I'd better get on. Derek's any trouble, send him out to me."

Derek was no trouble. He was sitting on the floor watching another cartoon, just as he had been in what seemed the distant days before she met Billy. Although he was not eating crisps as he had often been then, his mouth worked convulsively, and occasionally a slight shudder passed through his frame. She sat in a chair near him and watched the screen. A cat was chasing two mice, and time and again just failed to catch them. The cat put some cheese on a piece of bread, placed it near a hole and waited, paw at the ready. On the other side of the hole one mouse sniffed the cheese, the other was getting a poker red hot in a coal fire. The two mice came out of the hole together, one going for the cheese while the other rammed the hot poker up the cat's backside. The cat leapt in the air and A-A-A-ARGH came out of its mouth.

Derek turned round and glared at her. "What you looking for? I don't want you looking."

She left him to the TV, said goodbye and see you tomorrow to Patty who was hoovering her bedroom and drove into town. Since Billy had said "Sorry, wrong number" it meant things were arranged, and he would be waiting at the Marvin at their

181

usual time, between four-thirty and five. It was now just past midday which left acres and acres, hours and hours, of time to fill in. Fill in, fill in, what a strange phrase, you filled in a crossword, how could you fill in time? The pain in her head had quite gone but she still had the feeling of being divided, so that half of her was somewhere else. This made it hard to concentrate on what she should do next, which was go to the bank, draw out money, have lunch, and then drive slowly to the Marvin and wait in their room, their private and personal room. But someone had hold of her arm.

"Mrs. Lassiter, what a bit of luck. I'm delighted to see you." Jock MacGregor's red hair flamed in the sun. "If you've five minutes to spare come into the office, I don't think you've ever paid us the honour of a visit."

Five minutes to spare, she thought, why I have fifty minutes to spare, and more than that before it happens, the event which will give you a real story for your paper. The *Wyfleet Mercury's* offices, into which she allowed herself to be led, were in a pretty little early nineteenth-century house just off the High Street, with a bow window which bore the painted legend "News and Views from All Around" beneath the name.

"Sit you down," MacGregor said, and shouted "Bertie." A red-haired young man appeared. "My son Bertie, Mrs. Lassiter. Bertie's a chip off the old block, but a better journalist than the old block ever was, eh, Bertie?" Bertie did not deny it. "Rustle up a dish of tea for us, eh, lad?" When the young man had gone he said, "He'll be spreading his wings that lad will, he'll not stay long in Wyfleet." She saw this happening quite clearly, Bertie ascending over the roofs of Wyfleet, wings waving goodbye, yet at the same time knew perfectly well where she was, in Jock MacGregor's office, hearing him say: "Now, Mrs. Lassiter, what do you think of the news?"

The news, what was he talking about? It was no delaying tactic, no attempted deceit, when she said she didn't know what he meant. She found it hard to follow his words because her mind was somewhere else, no longer with flying Bertie, though she could not have said just where her mind was and what she was thinking of. When the tea came, in thick slightly stained yellow mugs, she tried to remember the last time she had been drinking tea. At breakfast? No that was coffee. She suddenly heard, part of her heard, what MacGregor was saying.

"Not often a local paper beats the nationals, but I had a call from the *Independent* this morning, they'll be running the story. What the *Mercury* says today the *Independent* prints tomorrow, eh? And, Mrs. Lassiter, I'd be most interested to know your reaction, how your husband took it. You've seen the paper? The news came at a lucky time for us, just managed an old-fashioned Stop Press item." The paper's front page said, COUNCIL CORRUPTION POLICE INVESTIGATION, but MacGregor's finger pointed to a few lines at the side in heavy type under the heading STOP PRESS. She read:

COUNCIL CORRUPTION

Leader of Wyfleet Council Richard Casement, local businessman John Hatter, builder Clive Braden and architect Victor Lassiter are the subjects of police enquiries into allegations that contracts for building work were given to Braden Builders although lower tenders had been put in, and that building permission had been given on several sites although not passed by the relevant sub-committee. Police have taken away papers from Mr. Casement's offices and those of the other businessmen involved. Further developments are expected. Read about them in the *Mercury*, your local paper.

She gave back the paper. She remembered now, of course, where she had last been drinking tea. It was in the TeasReady at Hastings. She saw Willem opposite her in his slightly shabby grey suit, the bits of dried blood round his jaw. Then he was metamorphosed into red-haired MacGregor, who had again been saying something from which she absented herself. She concentrated on his words.

"I rang your husband, Victor, this morning, but he was too busy to speak, and the others involved wouldn't talk to me except for Johnny Hatter, who said the stories were all bloody nonsense. Now, that's not the way to go on, if you let your case go by default, all sorts of rumours are bound to spread. So I'm asking you, in your own interest, to give me a story, tell your side of it. There does seem to be a pattern in these contracts, you see. Casement gets building permission through, Johnny Hatter buys the land, Braden and your husband are builder and architect. I wonder if your husband, Victor, has ever talked to you about it?" She said Victor hardly ever spoke of business affairs, she knew nothing about it.

MacGregor nodded. "I understand the police were at your house. That must have come as a shock." She agreed. "Any idea what they were looking for, what they took away?" Papers, she said, but she had no idea what papers. "Papers, yes. I understand they took cartloads of papers and files from the various offices, van loads I should say perhaps." He laughed heartily, and asked about Victor's reaction. Unconcerned, she said.

"A very calm temperament, would you say? Then how about yourself? Would it be right to say you were outraged by the intrusion?"

She delayed so long in answering that he repeated the question. Then she said she supposed the police did what they had to do. She was trying to remember what Willem ate in the TeasReady. A toasted teacake, but what else? She remembered and said, "Welsh rarebit."

"What's that? I didn't catch."

"I was remembering something. I have to buy some cheese for supper, I must go now."

He showed her to the door, saying she could be sure the *Mercury* would report everything without fear or favour. Then she was in the High Street again, still with much too much time to spare. She considerd visiting the charity shop, but instead went to call on Debbie.

The Hatters lived at one end of the High Street, in what had been a warehouse, bought by Johnny and converted into a town house, with a garage and a games room on the ground floor, a living-cum-dining room and kitchen above, bedrooms on the top. There had been a fuss made at the time over the change from business to residential use, but the conversion had been done quickly, and the arguments faded away. Had Victor designed the change from warehouse to desirable residence? That was one of the things she couldn't remember.

"Am I glad to see you. I'm so bloody *miserable*." Debbie had a wide-eyed look, as of one waiting for something awful to happen. She led the way upstairs. "I'm having a drink, only thing to do when you're miserable, a little drinkie helps." Sunlight cut the big room in half. Judith sat in the sunny half, in one of the white hide chairs, accepted the gin Debbie gave her and said she had been drinking tea with Jock MacGregor.

"That rat, what in the name of God were you doing talking to him?"

"I didn't talk to him, he talked to me. I hardly spoke. Anyway, he's not so bad. Do you know his son Bertie?"

"I don't think so, should I?"

"He'll soon be flying."

"Flying?"

"Flying off to London. His father says."

"You sure it's only tea you've been drinking?" Debbie, small and dark, lay curled on the white sofa like—what?—a cat. "That bastard's muddied the water, caused half the trouble with the rumours he'd been printing. And we are in trouble, my love, believe me we're in trouble."

"About Nethersole?"

"Nethersole nothing. He's a pest but not important, we'd have got around that one way or another."

"By blackmail?" The gin had a good satisfying bite as it went down. "Victor admitted it. I said I don't approve."

"Hey there, whose side are you on?" Debbie looked at her glass in surprise. "Empty, how did that happen? Can't believe that, you need a refresher too." She refreshed both glasses. "I don't think you understand. We're all in trouble, not just Johnny, through that bugger Notley. It was Notley stirred everything up in the first place."

Notley, who was Notley? She felt detached from it all, half of her floating away, floating or flying. Don't fly away, the other said, stay here, come back to earth. "Don't know Notley."

"You must have heard of him. Chief Executive of the Council, resigned last year, the *Mercury* was full of it."

"Don't see the *Mercury*." A phrase occurred to her. "I know not Notley. Never knew Notley."

"You've missed nothing. How he ever got appointed I don't know, came highly recommended Johnny said. If we'd known a bit more what he was like he'd never have got the job. He was nothing but trouble from the start. Dick tried to get along with him, but it was no good."

"Dick?"

"Dick Casement."

"The rabbit. The nose twitcher." She tried to make her own nose twitch. Debbie laughed, kept on laughing. They both did nose twitching.

"You're good for me, you know that, Judy. Don't know why, not got that much in common, but *you are good for me*." She shifted position on the sofa, looking more than ever like a sexy cat. A *sexy* cat, always looking out for it, what had she said about Billy, called him dishy. Judith wondered why she hadn't realized before what was suddenly clear to her. She broke into what Debbie was saying.

"You've been to bed with Billy."

"Who? What are you talking about?"

"Billy Gay. My driver, the refresher course. You said he was dishy, you've been to bed with him."

"Oh my *Gawd*." It was evidently enough to make a cat

laugh, and this cat did laugh, discreetly as cats do, almost soundlessly. "You really thought—that baby-faced boy—darling, I don't go for cradle-snatching, I like something more mature. He wasn't the one I meant, it was my driver on the course, Conan, a lovely Irishman with that bold look in his eyes they have. Not that I did anything *of course.*" The cat giggled. "And you really thought—*you've* been to bed with him."

See what you've done now, the other said, opening your mouth too wide. But leave it to me. She did leave it to the other, and admired the coolness with which she told Debbie not to be ridiculous, she was devoted to Victor and he to her, only that morning—and she repeated what Victor had said that morning about being in harmony. Was Debbie convinced? Perhaps, though there seemed still to be a gleam of doubt in the cat's eyes. But still, she left the subject of what either of them had or hadn't done, and returned to the trouble they were in.

"You're right about Dick, he does look like a rabbit though I never noticed. Mind you, he's not, don't you believe it, Johnny said to me you don't want to get on the wrong side of Dick Casement. What was I saying?"

"Notley."

"Notley, right, right. You know what I'm going to do, make us a sandwich. I tell you what there is, you tell me what you'd like. There's ham. And there's tuna. And cucumber. Ham and cucumber, tuna and cucumber, which?"

"Suppose I said ham and no cucumber?"

"Ham and *no* cucumber. You make me laugh, Judy, you really are good for me. Ham and cucumber, I don't know." She refreshed their glasses for the second or perhaps the third time. "I was telling you about Notley. Johnny has a feeling about these things, he said to me the first time he saw him, he said Notley, he's going to be awkward, that's an awkward one you've got there, Dick. But would Dick listen? Would he hell. Dick says leave him to me, I brought him in and I'll put

187

him out. If I have to, Dick says. He says I've brought more awkward ones than him to heel—"

"To heel?"

"What's wrong with that?"

"A rabbit bringing someone to heel." They both laughed at that. "You know what, I might have liked him."

"Dick?"

"Notley."

"You never *met* Notley, how could you have liked him? And take it from me, Notley's been the stinking smug interfering bastard who started all the trouble. And something else, you know what he does? He uses some stuff on his face or *somewhere*, you can smell him a mile away."

"He's a skunk."

"Of course he's a skunk. So how could you like him?"

She agreed she couldn't like Notley, but she felt a need, or the other felt it, to say no to Debbie about something. And there was something else, something she should be doing, but her mind was—a blank? Not a blank, more like a maze in which she had taken a turning that led to this house, this room, Debbie. She said, "I don't like this house."

"That's a hell of a thing for my best friend to say."

"Don't mean that, not exactly. What I mean is—" She took another drink, and was surprised to see a little splash on the black carpet. "—I don't like my house."

Debbie nodded, a wise cat. "That roof. It's a bit much." Judith nodded in agreement. "Much too much. But nothing to do with this house, no green tiles here."

"I like this house." After all, Debbie was her best friend, her only friend. She didn't want an argument.

"Good. Very good. About Notley. He poked his nose in. Dick bent over backwards." Debbie bent backwards herself, uncoiled, retained her position on the sofa precariously. "But in the end he had to go, with a golden handshake. But was he satisfied? Some people are never satisfied. He's been gunning for Dick and Johnny ever since."

She was in the middle of the maze and had taken a wrong turning, nothing visible but avenues of green, no indication which way to go, move to the end of one avenue and you were confronted by an identical one running at right angles. Confusing, she said, or perhaps didn't say. What was that, she asked, what did you say?

"Never did anything people aren't doing all the time," Debbie cried. "Setting up a holding company, everybody does it, the auditor said all right. Dick was never a partner in the holding company, he had a nominee, it was all just a way of cutting out red tape, getting things done. Trouble with this country everyone knows, can't get things done. Council used to take months to reach a decision, everybody knew that, Victor knew it, must have told you." Judith shook her head, but Debbie seemed not to notice. "Victor knew, knew as much as Johnny and Clive, all went smooth as could be, doing nicely, and who was getting hurt? Nobody getting hurt, nothing would have gone wrong except for Notley. Dick tried to bring him in, and that was a mistake. Notley's been gunning for him ever since."

She felt her eyes closing. Sunlight beat on her lids, warming one side of her face, leaving the other cool. Debbie got off the sofa, came over, shook her.

"Don't you realize they can all go to *prison*? Johnny's out of his mind with worry, Victor must be too."

"Victor says . . ." she began, but lost the thread.

"Yes, tell me. What does Victor say?"

"No need to worry. Fuss about some contracts, is all."

She heard Debbie repeat *all* scornfully, but the intense need to close her eyes blotted out further words although she was aware of their existence, aware of something not done, or not said.

5

She woke with a headache. On the white sofa Debbie, coiled like a cat again, snored. The gin bottle stood beside her on a glass table, empty. Judith went out unsteadily to the bathroom, looked in the glass, said "Something the cat dragged in," took off her watch, washed her face and hands, looked in the bathroom cupboard and found a bottle of tablets called Loozpain, swallowed three with a glass of tap water, put on her watch again, looked at it. A quarter to four. She must have been asleep for more than two hours. A moment later she looked at her watch again. A quarter to *four*. The bank closed at three-thirty.

Her actions in the next minutes were coherent, sensible yet the fruit of panic. She thought of writing a note for Debbie, abandoned the idea when she couldn't find paper, ran down the stairs, banged the front door. The bank was no more than a couple of hundred yards away down the High Street and she ran there, remembering that some branches now stayed open until four-thirty. But the doors were uncompromisingly shut, and although she rang and rang at a bell beside the door, nobody answered.

A middle-aged man wearing a sporty jacket, grey trousers and highly polished brogues said sympathetically, "Scandalous. No use ringing, they're inside but they won't answer, supposed to be working." He waved a malacca cane. "I've written to the manager." He coughed. "May I be of assistance in any way?"

She thanked him, said untruthfully that it was perfectly all right, looked again at her watch, and thought she might possibly find Billy at home before he set out for the Marvin. The Fiesta took her to Primula Street. The beat-up Vauxhall Astra stood outside number eighteen. Her watch said three minutes past four. Billy answered the door. He wore old cotton trousers and a string vest.

She was so eager to tell him what had happened that she did not notice whether he was surprised or disconcerted by her appearance at the door as she said, stumbling over the words, that the bank was shut, she hadn't got the money, could get it early in the morning. Only when she had told him this did it occur to her that she was still standing on the doorstep. She asked if she could come in.

"Okay," he said. "Yeah, okay. For a minute." In the front room, back to the plaster dogs, he said, "Five minutes I'd been gone. I'll give Willem a bell, get hold of him somehow. Morning should be all right, yeah."

Only then did it strike her that he was uneasy, wanted her gone. She asked what was wrong.

"Nothing. You been drinking?"

"Oh." Was it so obvious? "I suppose—yes, I have. Fell asleep. I'm a little bit—off beam. But something's the matter, what is it?"

"I said nothing." It was the first time she had seen him show irritation. "Didn't expect you to be half cut is all. You'll have the dosh in the morning for sure?"

"The dosh? Oh, the money. Yes, for sure."

"Or it's off, he'll be away, you know that?"

"I said in the morning." Suddenly she knew. "You've got somebody here, haven't you? Upstairs. A girl."

"Course not, it's only—"

"Yes?"

"My mum, she's shopping, be back soon. Sees you here again, you're supposed to be a client, what'll she think?"

"Does it matter?"

"You ain't got to live with her. Don't know what she's like." Upstairs somebody was moving around, a door closed. Billy jerked a thumb. "Lodger. She's let the spare room—does sometimes, some poxy commercial traveller. Left his case outside there, 'spect you saw. About tomorrow. All right if I come up to your place half ten? See I got to meet him around eleven, check it all out, if it's okay, give him the dosh."

"And then he telephones—"

"Dunno about that, don't wanna know. You neither. This'll be the first half, s'pose he asks about the second, when's he getting it?"

"I've settled that with him."

"Okay, okay, we're set. Better go now before my mum comes back. Half ten tomorrow."

There was no doubt about his eagerness to get her out of the house, and she noticed that there was a suitcase standing just inside the door. On the way back to Green Diamonds she wondered whether it was really a lodger upstairs or some girl from the Estate, and decided she didn't mind much if it was a girl. Did she really love Billy Gay, the other asked her, was it possible she could put up for long with a yob who said *You ain't got to live with her*? Let's face it, the other said, hasn't Billy Gay been the means to an end, to the understanding of what you're really like, what you really want, who you really are? The words stayed in her mind during the hours afterwards spent listening to Victor, sitting opposite him that evening in the better of Wyfleet's two French restaurants, half-listening

while he talked amusingly enough about the ridiculous questions he had been asked during his hours with the police, half-
thinking that in two or perhaps three days she would be free,
her own person, able to go where she wished, do what she
liked. Somewhere in her head, pushed to the back but not
extinguished by the Loozpain, lay the headache, which was
still with her when Victor said, "Another good evening, we
do get on don't we, as long as we leave s, e, x out of it," and
kissed her goodnight, warmly but decorously.

6

In the morning the conclusion, inexorable, yet by her unforeseen.

First rising. Then not the last supper but the last breakfast, butter pats curled, honey and home-made strawberry jam bought at the charity shop, coffee on the hotplate, her dark brown toast. As she put some strawberry jam into a pretty heart-shaped dish she wondered how much of it would be eaten. Then Victor bouncing in, full of dash, his bow tie scarlet and grey, suit grey with a faint fleck in it that might be red. The croissants pronounced perfect, the jam a touch too sweet, a day for honey.

And a day for conferences, Victor said, one in the morning with Johnny and Clive, then a long round table session with Nick Williams in on it. Not rabbit Casement, she asked, and Victor covered one clear blue eye with a wink and said from now on Dick would stay entirely in the background, an honourable councillor who had done no favours and of course been offered no reward. Let them prove otherwise, said Victor with fine confidence. He asked what she would be doing

194

today, nodded when she said this and that and then the charity shop, and said he would call her later. As she saw the Lagonda go down the drive she wondered if she would ever hear his voice again.

Today her head was clear, her mind undivided. If the other lurked somewhere, that did not disturb her, although it occurred to her that perhaps she *was* now the other and that Judith had flown away like Bertie MacGregor. But whether it was Judith or the other (and what was the difference really?) who answered the telephone when Debbie rang, she managed just the right tone of regret and friendliness when Debbie complained at being left so summarily and at the same time apologized because she felt she had been a bit over the top. She said she felt sure Debbie was worrying needlessly, added that Victor had been cheerful that morning, although (a nice touch in view of the disappearance to come) he had said he was meeting a man later who might have some important information.

She dressed for some reason with more than usual care, putting on a silky blouse the colour of which had been called azure in the shop, and a dark blue skirt. Checkbook in handbag ready for drawing the money, Victor's passport also in handbag to be given to Billy, who would pass it on to Willem.

Then something wrong. Patty's unmistakable voice calling her name, but this was not Patty's day. That clear undivided mind warned her of danger. Billy was coming at ten-thirty, Patty knew him, mustn't see him. Patty as always was full of words.

"Not my day I know, should be tomorrow, but tomorrow see Rocky says he'll take me and Derek to Dreamland at Margate, day after that he's off to Vienna then somewhere in Hungary or is that where Vienna is? Anyway, away a week so thought it'd be okay today—"

She interrupted the flow to say she was sorry but today was impossible, she had friends coming in this morning and didn't want any cleaning done. Patty was visibly offended or at least displeased, said okay but she didn't know whether she'd be able to come again this week, her mum was coming at the weekend, and she'd brought some photos to look at of her on the Costa del Sol at Easter, photos that, she said reproachfully, Judith had specially wanted to see.

Could she have said that? But good cleaners were rare, and she did not want to lose Patty. She looked at her watch, which said nine-five, saw she had plenty of time to get to the bank and back before ten-thirty, and sat down at the kitchen table while Patty ran through the photographs with explanatory detail.

"That's the view from our apartment, see, it was almost on the beach, just had to cross the road. Here's Derek with one of those funny hats the police wear, and that's him crying because they'd sold out of ice cream. Me and Rocky on the beach." Rocky looked like his name, a hulking beetle-browed figure towering over Patty. "We all got on so well, him and me and Carl." So Carl came too? "Yeah, he didn't have nothing on, see, thought he might as well come, brought some girl called Jessie, they went off on their own a lot, don't know if I got any pitchers of them, yes, here's a couple, see, here he is with me and Rocky. What's up, you all right?"

She said yes, but she lingered over the photographs to make sure that the unbelievable was true, and Carl was the man she knew as Willem. She was aware of Patty saying now Rocky was back Carl was staying with that boy she had driving lessons from and they was very thick, but what she really heard was the other asking what she had expected of a loutish treacherous young man with a criminal record like Billy Gay.

AFTERWARDS

So it was just a scam," Ewbank said. "Nothing more intended. No violence."

"Just a scam." Craxton's lips were tight. Three hours with Willem, otherwise Carl, sometimes called the Actor, real name Arnold Lippman, had given them the whole story.

"She hands over the cash and they tootle off abroad and spend it. They'd never have got away with it."

"Why not? What was she going to do, come to us and say look, they promised to kill my husband and didn't mean it?"

"Three thousand smackers." Ewbank shook his head in disbelief. "He must have spun a good tale. Or isn't she all there?"

"He's been an actor, maybe this was his best part. His idea, of course. And the other one, the little rat, he played his part pretty well too. He really fooled her. She was in love with him, or thought she was."

"In love. Oh ah, I've heard of it."

"You may be right at that."

"How d'you mean?"

"Maybe she's not quite all there."

Ewbank chuckled. "It must have shook them when Mrs. L called at Billy's home with his pal staying there and in a room upstairs, and Billy's mother liable to come back any minute and say something that blew the whole thing. If she'd found out then—"

"But she didn't."

It struck Ewbank that his governor was uncommonly short this morning. He changed the subject. "How's the fraud enquiry going, will they make it stick?"

"Not my pigeon, I only know what they tell me. Casement's up to his neck, spent a fortune on that tart Verna Upwood, set her up in a flat. Hatter too, very careless with papers, Hatter. Braden and Lassiter, they may get away with it. Or so they tell me."

"What about the photographs?"

"Nothing to it, they call it consenting adults. As you know." He said to the driver, "First right, up the slope."

They pulled into the drive of Green Diamonds. Ewbank looked at the gleaming roof in awe. "That's really something. Original." Before going to the house they examined the cars in the garage. There were dark stains on the passenger seat of the Fiesta. On the floor was a bundle of brown paper that had been done up with string, bits of old newspaper inside it.

"The dibs," Ewbank said. "She hands it over, says here's the money, he takes it, then bang bang goodbye Billy."

When Victor came to the door he recoiled momentarily. Craxton said, "It's Mrs. Lassiter we've come to see."

"Yes." Victor's hand went to his moustache. "I'm worried about her. Perhaps I should have been in touch before."

"When you saw the revolver had been found, you certainly should. It was yours, right?"

"It belonged to my father. I missed it, but just couldn't believe—"

"Where is she?"

"In her room. She spends most of her time there, didn't

198

come out to make my breakfast. You won't upset her, will you?"

The Sergeant snorted, perhaps with laughter. Craxton said, "You know why we're here." He walked down the corridor. Victor followed, pointed to the door. Craxton turned the handle. The door was locked. He said, "Open up. It's Craxton. Jack Craxton."

There was a sound from inside between a squeal and a yelp. The door opened. She stood there, wearing a flowered dressing gown, a blue nightdress beneath it. Her eyes were brilliant. "I knew you'd come. I've been waiting."

Craxton said nothing. She took hold of his arm. "I know where we can go, a little hotel, rather sordid but you won't mind that. I find I rather like it. The boy was a mistake, you know. I was really angry when I found out the trick they tried to play on me, but that's over now. I'm still just a little bit off beam, but you said you liked that."

She went on talking after Craxton had turned away, leaving Ewbank to read out the charge to her, that at some time on the morning of the twenty-fifth of June she had shot and killed one William Harold Gay.

It took the other a little while to realize what was happening, but then she fought all the way to the car. When she was inside, it took the two of them to hold her down.